Second Chance

by

Martha O'Sullivan

ISBN: 978-1-7367667-0-5

Second Chance

Cover by Charmaine Ross

Formatting by coversbykaren.com

To my husband Dan for making
all my dreams come true

The Chances Trilogy
By Martha O'Sullivan

Second Chance
Chance Encounter
Last Chance

Christmas in Tahoe (Coming in November 2022)

Visit marthaosullivan.com for summaries,
excerpts and more.

CHAPTER ONE

IT WAS ONLY BECAUSE he was here again that she kept crossing his mind. He was long over her, Brian Rembrandt reminded himself with borrowed conviction, imbibing the brisk mountain air. All he needed was a stiff drink, a thick steak and a dealer having a bad night. He wasn't much of a gambler, but the cards would occupy his ruminating mind. And no matter how tired he was, he could still count to twenty-one. Pushing down the past, he crossed the street under a cloak of pine trees draped in velvety, gray light.

He knew the way.

This wasn't his first time in Lake Tahoe, especially on the Fourth of July. Summer before last, he and Lindsay had watched the fireworks illuminate the basin here before making some sparks of their own on the beach. Lindsay had always wanted to make love on the sand, when the night was still but for the aspens whispering in the breeze and the occasional swoop of a gull's wings.

Brian had been happy to indulge her. Several times.

"Good evening, sir," the hostess greeted.

"Good evening." Brian replied, stepping through the threshold of the huge mahogany doors. The floor-to-ceiling window wall gave way to a panoramic view of the lake cradled by the Sierra Nevadas. "Rembrandt for dinner."

"Yes, Mr. Rembrandt." She consulted the chart on the podium, then directed him to the lodge-style restaurant at lake level. "Right this way."

He began to oblige, but stopped midway down the stairs, momentarily mesmerized by the breathtaking fusion of pastels coaxing the crimson sun into the inky lake. So much so that when he resumed his stride, he inadvertently collided with someone. Careening on the staircase as if in slow motion, she attempted to grasp the banister for ballast. Instinctively, Brian hooked the waist of the woman half his size and pulled her to him. The force of his reach threw them both into the corner of the landing. "I'm so sorry!" he exclaimed, mortified.

She shook back a mane of blonde hair, revealing porcelain skin and a glossy mouth parted in surprise. And cobalt eyes that twisted Brian's stomach muscles into braided dough. He lost his breath. "Lindsay?" Her name catching in his throat, he stroked her cheek with the back of his free hand, holding her eyes in his for fear blinking would make her disappear. "My God, Lindsay." Their faces were so close together that the air her sharp breath took in had no doubt been in his lungs first. She gaped at him, as if she'd seen a ghost, as all color drained from her face. Heart beating out of his chest, Brian gulped back the shock and righted them both, taking her hand in the process. It felt soft and damp, like a morning rose. Or maybe that was his palm sweating. After a shared moment of inertia, he asked, "Are you all right?"

She gave him a slow, affirming nod. "Brian." Her voice was barely above a whisper. "What are you doing here?" She took her hand back and lifted her chin a notch.

His gaze seemed tethered to hers. "Putting out a fire."

Brows knotting, she narrowed her eyes. "A fire?"

"Work." Brian finally shook off the stupor. "Long story."

A knowing smile curved her lips, but went no farther. "Oh."

He wondered if she meant to sound that disappointed. "I can't believe you're here. I was just thinking about you."

That seemed to surprise, then please her. Her mouth opened, but before she could articulate the thought, a man wearing a puzzled expression and a concerned frown arrived. "Linds? You okay?"

She swallowed the words, but her gaze remained fixed on his. "Yeah. I just lost my balance for a second." She paused, then added, "Paul, this is Brian Rembrandt. Brian, Paul Webster."

Brian tore himself away from her and extended his hand perfunctorily. "Nice to meet you."

Lindsay's companion met his firm handshake head-on. "Likewise."

"Are you visiting your grandmother for the holiday weekend?" Brian returned to her, biting back the urge to break the arm now girdling Lindsay's waist.

Her face clouded and her eyes hinted of tears as she shook her head from side to side. "She passed away last year."

Her irises were like bottomless pools, Brian reminded himself. And he suddenly found himself at risk of drowning. "I'm so sorry," he told her from the heart. "I know how much she meant to you."

"She did indeed." Her tone was wistful. "She was my only family."

Silence hung over them for a few steady beats. Then her companion cleared his throat and broke it in an even voice. "Our food has probably arrived by now. We should get back to our table."

Lindsay's gaze seemed to hold his a moment longer than she liked. Then she shifted her attention to her date and responded graciously, "Yes, of course. I never made it to the ladies room, though." She excused herself and started up the stairs.

Brian found himself reaching for her. "Lindsay."

She finished taking the step, then stopped. "It was nice to see you, Brian," she tossed over her shoulder, swallowing hard. "Good luck with those fires."

Brian could do nothing but watch her walk away in stunned silence. Then his gaze drifted to Webster and a tacit message passed between them.

With a superior smile and a chuckle in his eyes, the other man pivoted on his heel and retreated.

"Mr. Rembrandt?" called a voice from below. "I can seat you now."

Brian turned his head and nodded to the woman not much older than his daughter. He made quick work of the remaining stairs and fell into step beside her.

She showed him to a high-top table in the bar area. "Just one for dinner, right?" she confirmed politely, removing the second table setting.

"Yeah," Brian confirmed around a grunt. "Just one."

*****

"Where are they?" Lindsay scanned the beach. Finally, she spotted them down by the shore. The man pointed her out to the little boy, who began running toward her. "Mommy, Mommy! We found sea glass! Isn't it cool? Is it like the kind you used to find when you were little?" the towhead asked, wide-eyed with wonder. Nodding adoringly, Lindsay gave the crown of his wet head a tousle, then addressed his father. "Time for lunch." He lifted the boy to his shoulders, then leaned down to kiss her...

Lindsay woke heaving shallow breaths. She sat up in bed with a shiver and rubbed away the goose bumps erupting on her arms. The soft breeze raised the curtains, inviting the moonlight to streak the thick planks of her bedroom floor. She got up and closed the window before sitting on the window seat and gazing into the predawn darkness. She hadn't had a dream like that in ages. Seeing Brian must have triggered it.

And that had been very real.

She could still feel his hand on her cheek, she thought, raising hers to the same spot as the dream turned inward. And the rest of him looked as good as his hand had felt; the chiseled cheekbones and strong, square jawline on his perpetually suntanned face. She'd run her fingers through that ash blonde hair, slept against those broad shoulders and lost herself in those strong arms countless times. He'd smelled morning fresh like he'd just showered and was dressed casually in khaki pants and a collared shirt. He was here on business, he'd half-explained. She'd barely heard the words for the ringing in her ears and the thudding of her heart. And the hope that danced within her when he said he'd been thinking about her.

She'd been thinking about him too. But that was nothing new; she'd thought about him every day over the last year. From the day she moved out of her apartment in San Francisco to the day she buried her grandmother. And, of course, yesterday when she'd found that yellowed, rectangular-shaped box in the attic. Now it was a new day, she thought, as the first bands of light fought the charcoal dim behind the mountains, and she was thinking of him still.

But that would have to change.

Soon she would be Mrs. Paul Webster, son of one of the most highly regarded oncologists on the West Coast. And his wife, philanthropist extraordinaire, credited for raising millions of dollars for the new pediatric cancer wing at Reno General Hospital. One that, coincidently, her architect son had designed. To whom Lindsay owed an apology.

She'd foregone the ladies room for fresh air while, unbeknownst to her, Paul was instructing the kitchen to box their dinner. Once home, she barely picked at her food and after exaggerating an aching head, begged off the fireworks. After Paul left, she poured herself a healthy glass of wine, sat on the upstairs deck and had a good cry as the night sky exploded with color. She'd considered calling Moira, but she would have insisted on driving up. She'd had a date last night, her first in months, and Lindsay had no intention of ruining it on the whim of a lovesick girlfriend.

She let out an acquiescent sigh and ran an equally resigned hand through her hair. Must the Mountain Chickadee be so damned chipper at this hour? From its incessant chirping you'd think it didn't have a care in the world. Envious, Lindsay grabbed her robe and went downstairs. Her bare feet cringed on the cold wood floor as she made her way to the kitchen. All was quiet on the lake. The fishermen weren't out yet, the tourists were asleep and it was too early for the locals to go about the business of life.

He'd been alone, she lightened, ladling a heaping scoop of grounds into the filter. If he was seeing someone surely she would have accompanied him here on the holiday weekend, even on short notice. Not that it mattered, she reminded herself, extending her left arm and studying her hand, soon naked no longer. The solitaire had belonged to Paul's grandmother and the smaller diamond her mother's before her. He'd added to the original stones and reset the aggregate on a traditional gold band. Down on bended knee, Paul had been distracted by the ring slipping off, sparing him the astonishment that had no doubt flashed across her face, short-lived as it had been. Because the more she thought about it, the more sense it made. She loved Paul, after all. They had all but grown up together, had the world in common, wanted the same things. He would be a loving, faithful husband and a devoted father. The coffee maker beeped, ending her incongruous flight of fancy. Doctoring her coffee, she headed upstairs to start her day. She'd chosen the dream over the man. So she might as well start living it.

CHAPTER TWO

THE LAKE GLISTENED LIKE a sheet of sapphire glass reflecting the limpid sky, its silky waves swishing concertedly against the shore. The scent of suntan lotion and pine straw laced the breeze and Brian could taste summer in the air as he walked through the sand and crossed to the neighboring beach.

More gingerly than he liked, he self-admonished.

He'd relinquished his table for two and taken his dinner at the bar. Only he ate too little dinner and drank too much Scotch. Which was why his mouth felt stuffed full of cotton and his head pounded like a jackhammer.

But that's not why he'd rescheduled his flight.

He looked on as the reason he had crouched at the shore, as if searching for something in the fawn-colored sand. After a few moments of running her hands through it, she brushed them off and stood. Instantly the quicksilver of Brian's heartbeat spread to his cock and ignited. He had feasted on those voluptuous breasts, slept wrapped around those dancers' legs and unsparingly indulged himself in everything in between. And last night all he could think about was Paul Webster doing exactly the same thing. Which was why he was standing on the beach sweating his ass off instead of emptying his pockets in Security right now.

He watched as Lindsay, oblivious to his lecherous contemplation, smoothed her hair and sat down. Sparing the phone on the chaise lounge a cursory glance, she tossed it into the mesh bag at her feet. She briefly considered the magazine that lay next to it before it saw the same fate. She reclined and within seconds her breathing leveled and her breasts began to move up and down steadily inside the clingy halter top. He wondered why she had done away with her sexy belly button ring.

Brian made his way to her. He stopped just short of her chair and shrouding her in his shadow, swallowed hard and found his voice. "Lindsay."

Her eyes flew open behind the Ray Bans she wore and her lips parted in silent surprise for a few blinks. Then, in a voice colored with awe, she sat up with matching consternation. "Brian."

Holding her eyes in his, Brian decided he didn't care if she was alone or not. He was going to say his piece. "May I?"

"Sure," she stammered, gesturing to the foot of the chair and scooting up to the top. Cocking her head to the side, she took him in. "You remembered this is my beach."

He hated that she found that so shocking. "Yeah," he told her. "I remembered." He sat on the edge of the cushion, mindful to leave a buffer zone between them. She was looking at him expectantly, as if waiting for him to speak. So he did. "What happened to you last night? You disappeared."

Again.

"Yeah." She sent a revelatory look out over the water. "I had to get out of there."

Brian felt the knot in his stomach tighten. "I waited for you to come back."

Again.

Her gaze snapped back to him. "You did?"

Apparently she found that as surprising as he had. "Yeah, I did."

She seemed to struggle to remain impervious, but a hint of satisfaction crept into her eyes. "Oh."

That relaxed him a little. "How have you been? Did you get through your thesis? Finish your MBA?"

The twinkle immediately faded. "No, all of that got shelved when Gram got sick. Pancreatic cancer can be very aggressive. Then I had to settle her estate, get everything in order. I'm just now turning my attention back to school."

Brian fought the recurring urge to take her in his arms and hold her until the doleful look in her eyes went away. Instead he kept his feet planted firmly in the sand and the palms of his hands glued to his thighs. "I'm sorry you've been through such a hard time. I'm even sorrier I couldn't help you through it."

Deep emotion had settled in her eyes now. "Thanks. Moira was with me every step of the way.

And Pa—" She switched gears midway. "And the Brodys collectively were great."

Brian's blood was starting to boil and it had nothing to do with the heat of the day. He clenched his teeth. "Can we go somewhere to talk?" Or dinner later, he thought but didn't dare ask. He didn't want to hear she had plans with Webster. When she didn't answer, he laid his hand on hers. "We could walk out on the pier and have a drink, watch the boats come in." He nodded toward the hotel pier a few hundred yards away. "I'm staying over there."

She considered first his face, then his hand resting on hers. "Let's talk inside instead." She swung her legs over the side of the chair and began gathering her things as if the matter had been settled. "It's time I went in anyway."

Brian nodded by way of reply and helped her up. As they fell into step together, trudging through the coarse sand, Lindsay shot him an oblique grin. "Wait until you see what I've done with the place. You won't believe your eyes."

*****

"Would you like something to drink? Beer, water, a soft drink? It's a little early for wine, but I have that too," Lindsay offered from her kitchen a few minutes later.

"I'm on the wagon today," Brian told her. "I'll take a water."

She grabbed a bottle from the refrigerator as Brian took in the kitchen. "The place looks fantastic. The frosted glass panels remind me of—"

"The place we rented in Napa," she finished for him incredulously, aware of the similarity for the first time. It was a wonder either of them remembered any room other than the bedroom in that vineyard cottage. She fastened another button on her tunic and cleared her throat. "Thanks. I wanted to maintain the vernacular feel of the house, but modernize. So I went with browns and greens, like the siding and the roof. The floors are original; I had them sanded and stained. For a darker contrast against the walls." She paused, watching Brian shift his steel blue eyes to the French doors leading out to the deck. A brilliant blue haze had settled over the basin, encompassing the lake and the mountains beyond. "But there's no competing with Mother Nature." His gaze cut back to hers and she saw the same uneasiness on his face that she felt in her stomach. "We decided to go with a peninsula instead of a table and chairs," she continued, struggling to keep her voice level. "Knocking out that area doubled the size of the kitchen."

"We?" Brian asked, shoving his hands into the pockets of his deeply creased shorts. His eyes rested on the red roses bursting from a vase on the granite island.

"Jack Brody, Moira's brother, and I. They did the remodel." Brian nodded in recollection, and she saw relief flicker in his eyes. It resurrected the guilty hope from the night before and curved the horizontal line she had planted on her mouth into an unintended smile.

They held each other impalpably for a few seconds until Brian, eyes reverting to the lake, observed, "The wind is picking up already. Tonight won't be as calm as last night." His regard returned to her and it reflected the double entendre of his words.

"No, it won't." Her stomach bit as she went to the sink and nervously began washing dishes that were already clean. She cleared her throat and tried to make conversation. "So, did you get those fires put out?"

"Temporarily." Joining her, Brian grabbed a dish towel. "Remember All Tech Software?"

"Of course. They were one of your biggest clients."

"Sacramento has a problem with the emissions from their plant near Fresno. Fresno being the breadbasket of the world, the state is particular to environmental code compliance there. The state shut them down last week," he elaborated. "We've worked out a thirty-day stay, but I'll have my work cut out for me when I get home."

Lindsay sighed inwardly, rinsing a bowl for the third time. It should feel odd to be standing with him here at the kitchen sink, doing dishes and chatting about the latest crisis at work. But it didn't.

And that was a problem. She almost had to remind herself not to ask what sounded good to him for dinner or what their plans were for the weekend. Instead she changed the subject. "How's Kelsey? She graduated this spring, right? I wanted to send her something but thought it might be awkward."

"She's great, starts at USC in the fall," Brian answered with a proud smile. "And it wouldn't have been awkward. She still asks about you." He paused, then finished quietly, "She says I was a fool to let you go."

Lindsay's hands froze under the water and her breath hitched, but she willed her eyes steady, trying to remain focused on the busywork. Until Brian turned her by the shoulders and taking her face in his hands, proclaimed, "She's right." His gaze fell to her mouth and after a long, poignant beat, he brought his lips to a whisper away from hers and hovered. She found herself barely able to expel breath, let alone move. She could only close her eyes in anticipation as he grazed her lips with his. Finding no resistance, he curved a hand behind her neck and pulled her to him. He laid his lips on hers and began to move slowly over them. The familiar taste and texture of him felt like coming home after a long journey.

His mouth was hot and hungry. Very, very hungry as if it hadn't eaten in eons. And when her lips alone weren't enough to satiate it, he parted them and placed his open mouth squarely on hers and plunged his tongue deep. He fed greedily, drawing all of her into his mouth and feasting little by little, bite by bite, until not a breath remained between them. Then with a spent sigh, he ran his tongue along her top teeth so sensually that she quivered with long forgotten dampness below. "Lindsay…" he mumbled her name as if he'd never said it before.

"Brian…" she heaved in kind.

"I miss you." He let out a jagged breath. "I miss us."

She let the joy of basking in Brian's arms again run through her, warm her. Until she realized *she was in Brian's arms again*. She sprang back, mortified by her visceral reaction, and braced herself against the bank of cabinets that lined the back wall of the kitchen. She had to put some space between them. "I can't do this."

"I'm sorry." Brian's voice was thready. "I wasn't trying to—"

"Don't apologize," she managed. She saw the lust brimming in his eyes now, but it was laced with something more. Something profound. She wondered if he was seeing the same in hers. Still, she shook her head. "You need to leave."

"The hell I will. We need to talk this through."

She opened her mouth, closed it again and drew a stabilizing breath. "There's nothing more to say. We had a wonderful year, but we want different things," she told herself as much as him.

Anger flashed across his face and crept into his eyes, replacing the vulnerability she'd seen in them. "It was a helluva lot more than a wonderful year and you know it," he countered, trudging a hand through his hair and starting to pace. "How could you just leave like that?"

Lindsay had asked herself that a million times. And the answer was always the same. She trailed him inertly. "Because I had no other choice. I had to be honest with myself. We had to be honest with each other."

"Why did it have to be all or nothing?"

"The longer it went on, the harder it would have been to let go."

"That's bullshit."

Completely unnerved now, she painted a stoic expression on her face and crossed the room. Standing her ground, she opened the door and repeated, "You need to go." Her tone was a complete contrast to the tears burning in her throat. "Please."

Brian sent her a resigned nod, then grunted in deference. "Fine. I'll go, but it's not over. Not by a long shot." Tipping her chin, he brought her gaze to his. "Because I'm not going to be able to stay away from you this time." He released her gently and walked out the door.

Shaking inside, she watched him cross the yard and take a few steps onto the sand. Then he stopped and faced her again. "Honesty, huh? I'll give you honesty. The most honest year of my life was the one I spent with you." He turned on his heel and walked down the beach in the direction of the hotel. Closing the door, she gave into her rubber-like knees and slid to the floor. She had, hundreds of times, told herself she'd done the right thing for her, for the both of them, in the long run. So why was she suddenly filled with such regret?

CHAPTER THREE

BRODY AND SONS CONSTRUCTION had relocated their office to downtown Reno a few years ago when the riverfront revitalization was in its infancy and the government incentives were too good to ignore. That worked just fine for Moira. She'd much rather be here among the boutiques and cafes than stuck in an industrial park on the outskirts of town. She did the books for the business and saw to the day-to-day running of things while her father and brothers were out in the field.

It was exactly what she'd promised herself she would never do.

She'd earned an accounting degree and wanted to be the CFO of something, anything, but Brody and Sons G.C. She wanted to live in San Francisco or L.A. or Chicago. But the housing boom had changed all of that. As had the economic downturn that followed. So she'd stayed. She'd modernized the office and computer systems, automated bill payment and increased efficiency while decreasing expenses. She'd hired and fired, wrangled with the county and even convinced her father to invest in going green. And somewhere along the way, she actually started liking it. It was the first thing she'd ever done all by herself. Something no one had taught her; she'd figured it out. Something to call her own.

Moira was alone in the office today; official-ly they were closed for the long holiday weekend. But Jack needed quotes run and people expect to be paid, holiday or not. If she finished early enough, she might call Lindsay and invite herself up to the lake. "It's hotter than hell down here," she muttered out loud, reworking her hair into the claw clip at the back of her head.

She didn't look up when the door chimes rang, assuming it was Jack or her dad. And they could wait until she hit send. She blew her side-swept bangs out of her eyes and turned around, momen-tarily unsettled by how pleasantly surprised she was to find neither one of them standing in front of her.

"Hey."

"Hey, yourself." Moira returned the greeting, pushing up from behind her desk. Paul was Moira's definition of conventionally handsome. If it wasn't his caramel-colored eyes and dark, wavy, hair, it was his olive complexion and athletic build. Was it her imagination or did he hug her longer than usual? Breaking apart, she cocked her head to the side and studied him. His face was as long as a sum-mer day and his eyes as sullen as a scolded puppy. Her smile plunged along with her stomach. "Did something bad happen? Is Lindsay all right?"

"I don't know," Paul answered flippantly, shrug-ging his shoulders. "You two finish each other's sentences. You tell me." He perched himself on the edge of her desk, one denim-clad leg bent at the knee, and looked at her sharply.

Moira was a terrible liar, never one to think on her feet. She threw her glance around the office, searching for an answer. And came up empty. "I don't know what you mean." She watched Paul cross the room and stare out the window at the waves of heat radiating off the pavement for a long moment. He was probably the only man she knew who could wear a pink polo shirt without looking the least bit feminine.

"Does Lindsay want to get married?" He started to say something else, but changed his mind and swallowed it.

"She said yes, so I assume so," Moira reasoned flatly, threading a pen through her fingers.

He spun around to face her. "Why?"

"Why what?"

"Why is she marrying me?"

Moira returned to her desk and started shuffling papers needlessly. "I guess because she loves you and wants to spend the rest of her life with you, Paul. Isn't that why people usually get married?"

He met her snarky look head-on. "Usually. But there are a host of other reasons. Convenience, financial security, procreation, companionship."

Moira watched the pain of these possibilities cross Paul's face and settle in his eyes. "Yes, I suppose there are all those reasons. But Lindsay has plenty of money, thanks to her grandmother. She's too young to worry about her biological clock and let's face it." Moria laughed around the words. "She's beautiful and doesn't know it, making her no stranger to male companionship." He was standing right in front of her again and she could smell the anise in his cologne. It ignited every cell in her body and forced her to concentrate on drawing breaths. She started to reach out to him, but thought better of it and slapped her hands against her thighs instead, asking, "Where is all this coming from?"

"Oh, I don't know," Paul began sarcastically. "Lindsay seems to have an excuse for everything lately, especially when it comes to the wedding. She's always gardening or busy or *something*." Waving his hand in the air dramatically, he finished in a low growl, "And you no doubt heard who we ran into last night."

She gave him an affirming nod. There was no use in pretending otherwise.

"Part of the reason she and Rembrandt." He spit the name out like a bitter pill. "Parted ways was because he didn't want to settle down, commit. So she is worried about her clock."

Moira wished she were anywhere else. She had Paul's undivided attention and had not a stitch of makeup on and had thrown her hair up right out of the shower. She scolded herself for self-indulging and conjured up a compassionate smile. "I think you're being paranoid, but to set your mind at ease, just ask Lindsay." As the words slid off her lips, she knew they would never come to fruition. Paul was too afraid of the answer to pose the question. He'd live with a shadow of doubt rather than risk an inconvenient truth. "She probably just needs some space. Everything is happening so fast."

Gaze lingering on hers, Paul shook his head up and down contemplatively. Then he waved off whatever he was thinking and flashed her that killer smile. "I know, I know. You're right. What would I do without you, Moirs?"

The irony of the guileless statement not lost on her, Moira smiled in spite of herself. "Live a perfectly normal life."

He chuckled uneasily, as if the thought returned and startled him. Then his eyes swept the office, seeming to notice they were alone for the first time. He took a step back and cleared his throat. "Want to grab some lunch? My treat."

They'd had countless meals together over the years of course, but that was before. Before the slow, unbidden epiphany. A realization Moira had shared with no one. Whenever she let it enter her mind, dread curled up inside her. Like it was right now. She justified her silence with guilt and reason. No one deserved a guy like Paul more than Lindsay. Paul would never feel that way about her anyway. She was his best friend's sister. She would put her feelings aside and get over it. "How about a rain check? I've got a lot to do here."

"Sure." Silence hung over them for an interminable moment until a series of soft beeps filled the room. Paul shifted his gaze to the phone on Moira's desk. "Well, I'd better let you get back to it."

"Yeah," Moira agreed more hurriedly than she liked. "Duty calls."

He wagged a playful finger in the air. "I'm gonna hold you to that rain check."

"Deal."

"See ya, Moirs."

"Bye," she said and watched him walk out to the parking lot under the cloudless desert sky.

*****

"Damn it!" Lindsay said to no one and blew the errant strands of hair out of her face. Determined to put her nervous energy to good use, she'd picked up some stacking stones at the nursery. Knees bent and back twisting, she was unloading them from the back of her SUV.

"They deliver this stuff, you know. They even have people who will lay it for you."

"Now you tell me," Lindsay replied curtly over her shoulder.

"Where do you want them?" Moira availed herself, grabbing a few bricks.

Nodding toward the white fir in the middle of the yard, Lindsay directed, "Over there. I'm starting with the big one."

Moira obliged and went back for another load. "You went with Montana flagstone, huh?"

"According to your brother, it's natural, durable and is readily available in my color scheme," Lindsay informed her, setting down her third pile. "Do you want gloves?"

"No, I'm fine."

The two women worked in companionable silence for over an hour, unloading the pavers and stacking them around the trees and flower beds in the front and side yards. Then Lindsay clapped the gray powder off her gloved hands saying, "That's good. I want the border to look random, not manicured."

"Thank God! My back is killing me."

"Consider yourself lucky. My next project is stepping stones down to the water."

"You're on your own there."

They were sitting down in the shade drinking from water bottles when Lindsay noticed the bathing suit ties around Moira's neck. "Oh no! Did we have plans to go to the beach today?"

"No," Moira answered, shaking her head of raven curls. "I just decided to come up. To make sure you were okay."

"I'm fine," Lindsay told her. "Why wouldn't I be?"

"Oh, I don't know. Maybe because you ran into Brian last night. Or because you sounded like you were bouncing off the walls on the phone earlier."

She shifted her emerald eyes to the lake, choppy in the late afternoon wind. "Then there was Paul stopping by the office this morning."

"Oh, is he working with you guys again?"

"No. Not yet, anyway," Moira qualified, then shared Lindsay's gaze again. "He's worried about you, about the two of you. He asked me if you really loved him, were marrying him for the right reasons."

Lindsay had to will her voice to sound natural. "And what did you say?"

"I told him to ask you."

Lindsay busied herself with brushing imaginary dust off her jeans as her lifelong friend read her mind.

"Don't worry. He won't."

She returned the presumptive stare. "Why would I worry?"

"Because you're talking yourself into this marriage. I know you and Paul have a history. And that he's madly in love with you, of course. But being in love with someone is different than loving them for a lifetime."

Later it would make sense that guilt registered on Moira's fair face and her eyes grappled with some dilemma, but for now Lindsay's subconscious discounted all of that. "I know. I do love Paul that way."

"If you say so."

Defensive now, Lindsay scooted back a little. "Aren't you the one who told me to stop second-guessing myself and move on?" she contended. "What's done is done and all that."

"I meant about Grace, about coming home to take care of her. That was before Paul proposed. And Brian reappeared."

Lindsay waved the logic away. "It's all the same."

Moira shook her head from side to side. "Your grandmother wasn't the real reason you left San Francisco." She hesitated, then sniffing the air, decided to go on, "And what are the chances of you and Brian being at Hues of Blue at the same time?"

"Coincidence."

"Or fate."

"Fate has not been very kind to me so far. I don't put much stock in it."

"No, I guess you wouldn't," Moira allowed. "Fate can be cruel, has been to you. But like you, it usually has a plan."

Lindsay was utterly confused. "A plan?"

"Whether you knew it or not, you thought Brian would come for you. You thought if you pushed hard enough he'd miss you, give up, give in."

Had she? Lindsay put on her best poker face and refuted briskly, "I didn't have a plan. But either way, he didn't, did he?"

"He didn't ride up on a white horse dressed in shining armor, if that's what you mean." Moira threw a frustrated hand up in the air. "But he did use every portal known to man to try to contact you, including myself. And practically bought out the flower shop in his building."

Lindsay huffed out a dismissive breath as Moira kept going.

"So to justify your behavior, you convinced yourself that he didn't really love you. When you were the one who qualified your feelings, attached the strings, not him."

"We were at a crossroads. I left him a note," Lindsay disputed weakly.

"Yeah, that must have been a great way to top off a long day at the office," Moira fired back. "It was for the best, I suppose. I mean, if you really loved him as much as you'd claimed to, nothing else would have mattered. You wouldn't have felt like you were giving up what you thought your life would be for him."

Lindsay swallowed hard and narrowed her eyes at Moira and her attempt to play the devil's advocate. "And if he really loved me, he would have found me, compromised."

"Compromise is a two-way street. Who's doing the compromising now?" Moira's tone was increasingly cryptic.

Lindsay went with her gut and met it. "Moira, do you have something to say?"

She considered a moment, then answered quietly, "I love you, Linds. I want you to be happy. But

I think you need to ask yourself why you ran away from Brian and why you're marrying Paul. I bet the answer is the same. And it speaks to something greater."

Losing herself in the lake for a few silent beats, Lindsay outwardly ignored the question, but banked it. Instead she informed Moira, "Brian was here this morning. On the beach."

Moira fought a smile, but her dimples betrayed her. "Really?"

Lindsay met her satisfied expression directly. "He didn't come for me. He was here on business."

"Tahoe, yes. The beach, no," she said, closing the small space between them. "No wonder you're stacking stones."

"Yeah," Lindsay told her, lightly tapping Moira's shoulder with hers. "When you didn't pick up I had to do something."

"Sorry. You wanna tell me about it?"

"I'll have to give you the condensed version." Lindsay gauged the sun's position in the sky. "I have to go in and get ready soon. Paul and I have a wedding."

CHAPTER FOUR

"MR. REMBRANDT," THE BARTENDER with the ruddy face and smiling eyes greeted. "Nice to see you again."

"Hello." Brian hesitated, then went for it. "Mac."

Nodding as if impressed by the the recall, Mac set a cocktail napkin down on the marble-topped bar. "Manhattan again tonight?"im

"I think I'll play it safe with a Stella." Brian answered, ranging a leg over the bar stool across from him. "Do I have you to thank for waking up in my room this morning and not on the floor of the casino?" Brian asked Mac's back.

"I don't think you would have made it to the casino. That's across the street." Mac corrected, serving the beer. "The staircase over there." He pointed over Brian's shoulder. "Is about as far as you would have gotten."

"My deepest gratitude," he said. "I haven't done that to myself in a very long time."

"And it shows. Did it work?"

Brian inclined his head and wrinkled his forehead.

"Getting drunk," Mac clarified. "Did it make everything better?"

"No," Brian admitted, playing with the label on the green bottle. "And I felt like shit when I woke up this morning. But you already knew that."

"Indeed I do. I'm an alcoholic."

Surprise rolled through Brian. "An alcoholic who tends bar?"

"When temptation is all around you, it doesn't seem so tempting anymore. I've been sober since '88; still go to AA meetings every once in a while. I've even recruited a few regulars in here." Throwing a surreptitious glance around the bar, he leaned forward and spoke in a conspiratorial tone. "Don't tell my boss. It's bad for business."

"I'll put it in the vault," Brian assured him with a chuckle. Then, taking a pull of the import, went on, "Sober for three decades. Impressive. How'd you do it?"

"I was forty, divorced, unemployed and broke. I called my brother in Sacramento for money. Instead he took me to an AA meeting. Takes one to know one, I guess. In retrospect, my call for money was really a call for help. I wanted to stop, but didn't know how. That's how I got to Tahoe," Mac went on. "I wandered up here that first sober summer and never went back. My management experience in corporate America started coming back to me once my head cleared. I've been running the bar here ever since."

Brian chewed on that a minute. "You never wanted to get back out there?"

"I thought about it, but my journey to sobriety taught me I drank to escape. Stress from work, marriage, finances. I didn't want to get into that vicious cycle again. After a while I got used to the Tahoe lifestyle," Mac finished with a shrug.

"No regrets?"

"Not really. My brother is gone and his kids are scattered around, living their own lives. I guess my only regret is not having a family. When I'm gone, it will be like I was never here. No legacy."

Nodding, Brain took another swig.

"How about you?" Mac asked. "What's your story?"

"I grew up in Orange County, the only child of a busy, widowed doctor," Brian started with a tired breath. "I went to Stanford and met my ex-wife. We got married too young and ended up having nothing but our daughter and our alma mater in common. She and Kelsey moved to her native San Diego when we divorced. I've been going back and forth between there and San Francisco for nearly fifteen years now." He paused, then beaming, finished, "Kelsey is my legacy; the greatest part of my life."

"I can see that. But none of that brought you in here last night."

"No," Brian acquiesced, looking down at the now half-empty bottle. "I ran into an old…friend unexpectedly. I wasn't prepared."

"An old friend or an old flame?" Mac asked knowingly.

Brian shot him an impish look. "Not much gets by you."

"I knew the Weatheralls, Grace especially, for years. I was sorry to see her go and so fast. Talk about the greatest part of your life." His thin mouth became a wide grin. "Lindsay is her grandmother's legacy whether she wants to be or not." Connecting the dots, he asked, "So, are you the guy from San Francisco who broke her heart?"

Brian took an astonished sip and murmured, "We broke each other's hearts."

Mac gave him a rule-breaker's grin. "Broken hearts can be mended. Even broken souls. I'm living proof."

"There's more to it than that. We wanted different things. Plus I've got more than a decade on her. I couldn't see myself starting over at forty."

Mac grunted that away. "I did. And I'll tell you one thing, this side of forty has been much better so far."

Sounds of entry ended the conversation. Mac excused himself to greet a couple who'd just arrived. Brian nursed the rest of his beer along with an ineffable trepidation that he just couldn't shake. Then he threw a few bills on bar, tipped his head at Mac in silent salute and decided to do something about it.

*****

It had been eight hours since Brian walked out the door and no matter how hard she tried, Lindsay couldn't push him out of her mind. She'd felt wonderfully helpless in his arms, drowning in his familiar scent, his intoxicating taste, his provocative touch. Even as her head lay against Paul's shoulder, she could taste each layer of Brian's stolen kiss. The sweet tentativeness at the beginning, then the propulsive hunger and the tender longing just before he pulled away. But that guilty pleasure wouldn't happen again. She loved Paul, she reminded herself as they left the dance floor. She could never hurt him that way. Marriage and motherhood would fill the void left in her heart. And guarantee she would never be alone again.

"Lindsay, you look positively stunning," Theresa Webster gushed. "I simply adore the shimmering white of the gown against your sun-kissed skin."

"Thank you, Mrs. Webster," Lindsay returned, embracing the petite woman. Paul had gotten all his features but his height from his mother. Tonight she wore a black sequin-covered dress that flattered her mature figure. "Likewise."

"You've got to start calling me Theresa. We're as good as family. I'm sorry this is the first opportunity I've had to say hello," she went on. "My sister is an absolute wreck. I should have insisted on planning the wedding from the beginning. Organi-

38

zation is not one of her strengths." She beamed at her son, then addressed Lindsay again, "Speaking of weddings, is there anything I can do to help? I know you want a small, quiet affair," she acknowledged a bit reluctantly. "But maybe I could arrange the caterer? I have so many contacts through my charity work."

Lindsay sensed the innuendo in the other woman's voice and responded accordingly. "That would be wonderful. I'm a bit overwhelmed, with everything happening so fast."

"Great. I'll be on the phone first thing Monday morning." Her gaze wavered again, then rested on the couple's joined hands. Her smile began to fade, but she caught it just in time. "Now, I've got to rescue whomever's ear your father has," she told Paul. "He can't stop talking about the survival rate of this new drug protocol. And that does not good dinner conversation make."

"We'll walk that way with you, Mom," Paul offered, stepping off to follow her with Lindsay in tow. "We need drinks anyway."

"You go ahead," Lindsay countered, pulling him back and planting a hard, fast kiss on the center of his mouth. "It's such a lovely night. I'll meet you on the beach."

*****

39

Lindsay slipped off her heels and sunk her toes into the sand. The wind had picked up, blowing her hair in hard streaks across her face and neck and spitting surf on her ankles. Shimmying the cocktail-length dress just above her knees, she sat in the cool strand and gazed at the silhouette of the Sierras in the distance. The mountains guarded the lake, the lake became one with the shore and the sky held them all in the palm of its hand. Why couldn't life be as beautifully simple as that?

But it wasn't, it never had been for her. Her parents' accident on that icy mountain road a quarter-century ago had seen to that. And now Brian's reappearance in her life had shaken her to the very core again. Not to mention that Moira was being less than forthcoming about what was really bothering her. There was clearly more on her mind than Paul and Lindsay's impending marriage. She knew Moira's date on the Fourth of July had been predictably inconsequential. She was particular when it came to men, seeing someone a few times and then breaking it off. Lindsay made a mental note to revisit the matter with her friend and moved on to Paul's mother. What revelation had come over her so suddenly and why had she so deliberately tried to hide it?

Looking out over the water at the twinkling lights of Incline Village, her thoughts returned to Brian. She should have told him she was engaged straightaway. Especially when he said he wasn't going to be able to stay away from her. *This* time, as if he'd forced himself to before. Apprehension and excitement wrangled in the pit of her stomach, tinged with guilty hope. She hated herself for not wanting him to, she fretted as her hand met an unexpected obstacle in the granular rough. She dug a bit, drew it out. Sea glass, she thought, inwardly nostalgic. The piece was incredibly flawless, as if created by man and machine instead of sea and sand. No sharp edges or cracks, oddly proportionate. A rare, perfect find—

"I guess the Santa Anas have blown north," Paul announced from behind, interrupting her musing. He handed her one of the two wine glasses he carried and sat down next to her. "Beach combing again?"

"What?" she answered, realizing she'd been fondling the whiskey-colored wedge in her palm. "Oh, no. It's sea glass. Moira and I used to spend hours searching the shore for chips like this," she explained, displaying the shard with a sudden shiver. "It's unusual to find such a perfectly shaped piece."

"Are you cold? Here." Jumping back up, he removed his suit coat and draped it over her shoulders. "Better?"

"Much," she told him as he returned to her. He was so genuine, so dear, looking at her with eyes full of love and trust. Trust that she didn't deserve.

But she would earn it back, if only for herself. "Thanks."

"What did you do with the pieces you found?"

"We'd make wishes on them, then wire them together and make makeshift bracelets." Squeezing her hand shut, she looked out over the water again.

Silence fell over them for a long moment and then Paul asked, "What did you wish for?"

She tilted her face toward his and looked into his eyes, searching for the soulful reflection of her own. "You," she heard herself whisper. "I wished for you."

His eyes narrowed and began to dance as his mouth curved into a grin. He tucked her into the nook of his shoulder. "Then I guess we both got our wish." Brushing her lips with his, he held his glass out in the air in front of them. "To us."

"To us," she toasted, clinking her glass against his. The wine slid down her throat, warming her insides as her dreams held her close. She felt his heart flutter against her chest, searching for an echo.

"I love you, Lindsay."

"I love you, too." I *know* I do.

*****

Tar-like darkness swaddled the basin but for a handful of stars peppering the sky. Lindsay leaned against Webster, sexy as hell in a dress that hugged every one of her curves just right. He was wearing a suit, so they must have gone somewhere other than dinner and a movie.

From his vantage point under the cluster of prickly Ponderosa pines, Brian watched Lindsay rummage through her purse with the mindfulness of a toddler on Christmas morning. Thoroughly exasperated, she handed the clutch to her companion, who immediately located what Brian assumed was her keys and unlocked the door. Within seconds, a light blazed in the living room, augmenting the faint amber glow Brian had been contemplating for the better part of an hour. He gave silent thanks she was home for the night as the icy ball in his stomach began to thaw. Brian's first inclination had been to confront them in the driveway, but common sense prevailed and he thought better of it. What would he do then? Get into it with Webster? Confess he'd been waiting for Lindsay like a stalker? He'd seen no evidence of a man staying in the house, so he decided to wait for Webster to leave. If he left.

When the door opened an interminable fifteen minutes later, Brian was still on his feet, pacing in the tiny clearing. He clenched his fists and ground his teeth as Webster and Lindsay exchanged a few words, then embraced. And when Webster's mouth came down on hers, Brian felt like someone had cut him open and eviscerated him. Brian looked on as Webster scanned the night curiously, clapping his hands in a semicircle. Then he glanced back at

Lindsay and shrugged his shoulders as if to dismiss a theory. Nodding in acknowledgement, she waited until his car was out of sight, then shut the door. Brian heard the locks catch, but the lights continued to burn.

In subliminal invitation, he convinced himself.

He forced his frenetic breathing to level as his hand tapped on the knotty pine door, but his heart still pounded like a wayward gong. The clicking of heels on the other side had it leaping out of his chest.

"Was there a bear after—" Lindsay stopped short and drew in a sharp breath. "Brian."

The dress allowed her breasts to peek out just enough for Brian to taste them with his eyes. Her hair spilled to her shoulders in sexy, sun-streaked waves. Her lips held the remnants of shimmer and he sneered inside, knowing where the rest of the gloss had gone. Her redolent perfume filled his senses in their proximity, intoxicating him with her scent. The same way his apartment used to smell after she'd stayed there. And his bed used to smell after she'd slept there. The way he used to smell after he'd held her. The way he wanted to smell tonight. So he didn't wait for her to ask him in.

*****

Brian measured her for a few blinks before bursting in with the force of a runaway train. But

Lindsay was too lost in the way he was kissing her for that to register in her mind. All she knew was when he pushed her against the wall, took her face in his hands and usurped her mouth, she had never felt so needed. Not wanted or loved, just needed. Desperately.

He released her lips and keeping her jowls in his hands, kicked the door shut behind him. His fiery eyes locked on hers again and Lindsay wasn't sure if he was seeking consent or issuing warning. She yielded to both by wrapping her arms around his middle and bringing him to her. Brushing back the wisps of hair that surrounded her face, he muttered something unintelligible before capturing her mouth again. Her hands traveled up his back and into his hair as his demanding tongue sought hers. She returned the greed and hunger, but somehow checked the need.

She loved having his eager hands on her, relished in feeling him virile against her as he nuzzled her throat, cupped her breasts. They moved predatorily over her back now, sowing impoverished seeds of want from the round of her shoulders to the tips of her toes. Insides ablaze and restraint nonexistent, her unspoken plea was for him to unbind the tie that bound the dress to her and take her hard and fast right there on the living room floor.

Instead he tore his mouth away and buried his face in her hair. "I saw Webster kiss you just now." His voice was strangulated, his breathing craggily.

"I wanted you to remember how it feels to kiss me before you went to bed."

"I never forgot how it feels to kiss you." The admission all but died on her lips. She was pressed tight against him, molded to his body like a beloved pair of jeans. She felt his sawed-off breaths level and become regular, eventually taking hers with them. Her stomach churned, then plummeted, but this time she didn't push away. Some invisible force kept her there, wrapped in his arms, heart fluttering and head spinning from the rush of it all.

"You can't tell me it's like that." His fingers wound through her hair, as his heartbeat ran neck and neck with hers. He held her there for a few moments more, then eased back. "Look me in the eye and tell me I'm wrong."

Lindsay tried to part her lips in protest, but couldn't. She couldn't look into his imploring eyes and tell him every cell in her body wasn't electrified, filling every part of her with the memory of his touch. That feeling him throbbing and hard against her made that longing settle in the triangle between her legs. She simply couldn't look at him and lie. So she didn't.

"That's what I thought." He released her and started to pace around the living room, raking his fingers through his disheveled hair.

Closing her eyes, she lowered her head and massaged her temples with unsteady fingertips. Sobriety was sneaking up on her, bringing with it a blinding headache. She felt his burning stare for a few more clicks before he answered her silent prayer and changed the subject.

"Where were you tonight?"

"A wedding." She lightened a little, lifting her head to meet his gaze. "Paul's cousin."

Nodding in understanding, he closed the small space between them. "No wonder you're tipsy." He brushed the back of his hand gently across her cheek. "You love weddings."

"I love weddings with you," she let herself remember out loud.

Their eyes held for a poignant moment until Brian said, "All right, then. Up to bed with you."

Lindsay felt her jaw drop. "Bed?"

"We'll continue this discussion tomorrow, when you are of sound mind." He led her up the staircase and down the moonbeam-lit hallway to the bedroom. "C'mon," he drawled, retracting one side of the comforter and discarding the mountain of decorative pillows. "I'll tuck you in."

CHAPTER FIVE

LINDSAY ROLLED ONTO HER back and opened one eye and then very cautiously, the other. Her head, the apparent bounty in a volleyball tournament, was surely splitting in two. She sat up slowly, promising herself she would never, ever drink again and cursed the bright summer sun. Surveying the room, she noticed a blanket and pillow strewn upon the couch in the corner. She sprung up, hand to heart, and realized she was still in her dress. And that Brian had stayed with her. The mortification rising inside her would have been enough to keep her cowering in bed, but for the rich, earthy aroma floating through the crisp morning air. She rose gingerly, stomach pulling in apprehension and appreciation and headed downstairs.

"You really need to do something about those creaky floors." Brian was standing on the bottom landing in yesterday's clothes, legs crossed at the ankles, with a wide grin on his face. It accentuated the crow's feet that framed his eyes and reminded Lindsay of wondering what color eyes a baby of theirs would have. The most perfect shade of blue, no doubt. He handed her the steaming mug in his right hand. "Good morning."

"Good morning." Lindsay imbibed the coffee, sighing dreamily as it slid down her throat. "Thanks."

"I sweetened it with honey. Does wonders for a hangover."

"I'll take the hive, then"

"You still look great if that's any consolation. Love the pjs."

Lindsay ignored his attempt at humor. "You stayed here, didn't you?"

His expression instantly collapsed. "Of course I did. I couldn't leave you alone like that. Plus," he hesitated, then finished quietly, "I'm still waiting for an answer."

"An answer?" she stalled, averting her eyes to the open deck door. A jet ski roared by, leaving a zigzag of foamy footprints in its wake.

"Yeah." He was so close to her now she could smell the morning on him. "Why did you run away?"

The pull in her stomach turned to angst. "I didn't run away," she countered briskly. "My grandmother needed me."

Brian tipped her face to his. "I needed you."

Her heart soared in her chest, but she bridled it. Not enough, she reminded herself. "I'm sorry. I shouldn't have ended things that way. I know that now."

"You can't end what's not over. And it's not over between us." Linking his arms around her waist, he brought her to him.

"It has to be," she managed, swallowing hard.

"It's not," he muttered, relieving her of her coffee and kissing her under the earlobe. The spot he knew sent a quiver coursing through her body that wicked between her legs, like it was right now.

But it would be the last time. The last time her head would slant, allowing his lips to devour her throat en route to her mouth. The last time their tongues would meet and part cohesively. The last time his hands would scoop her up at the buttocks and she would instinctively coil her legs to circle his hips and her arms to wreathe his neck. The last time her pelvis would press against his urgency. Because somehow she would learn to live without his scent, his touch, his weight on her. Again.

Insides blazing, she went boneless as he carried her to the couch. His hands crept up her back, fumbling with the knot at her neck. She felt the ties of the halter fall into the valley between her breasts. Pangs of molten desire flooded her stomach as Brian suckled one breast, then the other. Straddled between his legs, she arched beneath him on the cool leather, scraping her nails up and down his back. She could feel his erection growing through the denim he wore. Sighing affirmations, his mouth left her breasts and his tongue meandered up her throat while his hands went to her hips, inching the dress down. Then the most primal of sensations began to quicken in the very essence of her.

"I don't think I've ever wanted anything more than I want to make love to you right now," Brian heaved.

"I don't think I have either." She shook her head from side to side, trying to clear her mind despite the heat steaming between their bodies. "But we can't. Because I'm getting married."

*****

"Married?" Brian was still on top of her, rising and falling with her shallow breaths. And hard as a rock. He had never been so aroused without making love before. "To Webster?" The words burned his tongue and he jolted back, blindsided.

Lindsay's nod was swift and, he told himself, the least bit reluctant. As if suddenly modest, she began pulling up her dress, struggling to tie it at the nape of her neck. "I should have told you before."

Brian sat on the edge of the couch and ran a dumbfounded hand through his hair "Yeah," he huffed out, "that would have been nice." He was thoroughly spent, all the life suddenly drained out of him. And his erection. "Why didn't you?"

"I don't know." She finished tying and stood, shaking the dress into place. "I guess." Her eyes went hollow. "I was afraid."

"Of me?"

She searched the air for the words. "No, of it. Once I tell you it's real. No going back."

It was frighteningly real to him already. Swearing under his breath, he stood and took her hands, grazing her fingers with his thumbs.

"It needs to be sized," she ground out with a gulp, reading his mind.

"When?"

"The setting has to be rebuilt so—"

"No. *When?*"

Her eyes softened with understanding. "We haven't set a date. Before the end of the year." She withdrew her hands and started to walk away.

Brian grabbed her arm. "Why?"

"Why?" Her expression was strained, puzzled.

"Why are you getting married?"

She took a deep breath, held it for a moment, then replied, "Paul and I have known each other forever. We want the same things. We are...familiar."

"That's qualified. *Why?*"

She had to think about that, which pleased Brian. "Because he asked me and there's no reason not to." She tried to shake him off, but he tightened his grip.

"I can give you a reason."

Her mouth parted slightly, allowing a short gasp of air to escape. "You can?"

He whirled her around and bringing their mouths within inches of each other said, "Yeah, I can." He could see the struggle in her eyes now but it was laced with hope, so he continued. "But first things first. Do you love him?"

"Yes."

That stung, especially since she didn't hesitate. "Did you run away because of him?"

She deadpanned him. "What?"

Narrowing his eyes, he clarified, "Did you leave me for him?"

She shook her head incredulously, as if those were the most far-fetched words ever been spoken. "No! Of course not. How could you think such a thing?"

"Why, then?"

"Brian, I didn't leave you. I left San Francisco," she explained, a preponderance of weariness coloring her voice. "We were unraveling. You didn't want to make a commitment; I couldn't go on without one. Gram's illness precipitated the inevitable."

"I was committed to you. There was no one else. I—"

"I know that," she broke in, as though needing him to know. "I mean marriage, a family. You'd already done that." Her shoulders stiffened as if to summon courage before she looked him straight in the eye. "It hurt too much to keep pretending."

"Were you pretending when we made love the night before you left? Or had you been pretending all along?" His attempts to stay hinged were proving increasingly ineffective.

Teardrops were gliding down her cheeks now, leaving behind threadlike, sooty tracks in their wake. "I couldn't have pretended that." She shook her head definitively. "Any of that. I mean pretending that we had a future."

"So you left, cut me out of your life and found someone to give you that future," Brian shot back, giving into his own anger.

"It wasn't like that. It just..." She settled on the word. "Happened. Paul was very supportive when Gram died." The pain was firmly etched in her eyes now, tearing at Brian's heartstrings.

"And I wouldn't have been?"

She dropped her broken gaze. "I wanted to call you a hundred times. But it wouldn't have changed anything. Other than both of us ending up even more hurt."

"It would have changed everything," he surprised himself by saying and tilted her chin to meet his eyes again. "The end of the year, huh? Looks like I got here just in time."

*****

"You want me to come to San Francisco next weekend?" Lindsay couldn't believe the very words she spoke.

"I'll send you a ticket," Brian offered matter-of-factly.

Lindsay backed up in astonishment and crossed the room, striving for calm. This conversation was absurd.

"The firm has a standing reservation at the Fairmont," Brian elaborated. "I'll hold a room in your name. Can you come on Friday and leave on Monday?"

"Brian, I can't visit you. I'm engaged!"

"Not officially." He went to her and clasped her writhing hands in his. "Promise me you'll consider it. You owe me that."

She supposed she did. "But Paul. What would I tell him? If it were the other way around…"

"Wouldn't you want him to be sure?"

"Yes, of course," she allowed. "But don't you have so much to do with the All Tech case?"

Waving away her attempt at another excuse, he repeated, "Will you come?"

"I don't know." She raised a troubled hand to her forehead. "I'm so confused."

"I'm not," Brian said, pulling her to him. His eyes were serious, his face resolute. "I told you. I'm not giving up so easily this time." Lindsay watched as a shadowy cast replaced the determination. "Unless you tell me there's nothing between us. That you feel nothing for me. Then I'll leave right now and you'll never hear from me again."

Wondering if he realized he wasn't exhaling, she moved her head slowly from side to side. "You know I can't do that."

"That's what I thought," he affirmed, his eyes sparkling triumphantly. "Think about where you want to have dinner on Friday night. I'll be in touch." Laying a kiss on her forehead, he consulted his phone. "But for now, I've got a plane of my own to catch."

CHAPTER SIX

BRIAN'S FLIGHT LANDED ON time, but traffic was horrific getting into the city. His arrival to Nob Hill proved to be just as colorful.

"Yeah, Mr. Rembrandt is home now." Saluting Brian, Mike Savoy spoke into the phone. "Sorry about the false alarm."

"What's up?" Brian asked his next door neighbor, scanning the apartment.

"Something must have triggered the alarm. I heard the siren and came in to check it out. I tried your cell."

Brian reached into his front pants pocket and retrieved his phone. "Still off from the plane," he informed him, rectifying the situation.

"Plane? Where were you?" Mike asked, nodding to the bag at Brian's feet.

"Tahoe."

"Tahoe?" Mike frowned. "Business or pleasure?"

"Both," Brian replied, grabbing two beers from the refrigerator.

"You haven't been there in a while."

"Tell me about it."

Mike sat down on one of the bar stools that lined the kitchen island and deftly twisted the cap off the import. "Okay. I'll bite. Did you meet a smoking hot babe who was so into you that the two of you ran away for the weekend? Or did Larry Ellison need some legal advice that his five thousand dollars-an-hour attorneys couldn't provide?" he teased, taking a deep pull.

"Close." Brian laughed in spite of himself. "The smoking hot babe is Lindsay and the client, although important to Cummings & Whitaker, isn't quite on Ellison's level. He doesn't own an island, just a software company."

"Lindsay?" Mike cocked his chestnut-colored head speculatively. "Hmm. Actually, I'm not that surprised. I never really understood why you guys split. She practically lived here and you had that look in your eyes."

"You and me both." Brian processed the words with a pull of his own. "What look in my eyes?"

Mike laughed without opening his mouth. "After countless brother-in-law candidates, I learned to recognize the look. I knew who my sisters were going to marry before they did. My mother says it's a gift." He paused with a slight bow of the head and goodwill beaming from behind his amber eyes. "Amended for you, of course. Seeing how you're not the marrying kind."

Brian decided to ignore the jab. "Why didn't you ever say anything?"

"I figured if you wanted to talk about it you would. Besides, you know my track record with women." He took in the room for affect. "So where is she?"

"In Tahoe. With her fiancé," he growled.

"Ouch. Who's the lucky guy?"

Brian brought Mike up to speed.

"You should be able to handle that. "What's your plan?"

With another healthy sip, Brian walked over to the window and watched Chinatown twinkle below. "What makes you think I have a plan?"

"You always have a plan. That's part of your problem."

"Not this time."

"You mean to tell me you spent two hours on a plane thinking about something else?"

His friend knew him well, Brian admitted to himself, watching the headlights reflect off the wet pavement. "I'm sending her a plane ticket for next weekend."

"Impressive. Bold move," Mike interjected around a swig. "But how will Mr. High School feel about that?"

"I don't give a shit. I only care about how Lindsay feels. She said she would think about it."

"That's encouraging." Mike leaned back with a skeptical grin. "If she were unequivocal she would have refused immediately. What's your strategy?"

"Strategy?"

"Yeah. What does this guy have that you don't?"

"Everything," Brian answered with a humorless laugh.

"I doubt that. But you have to play up your strengths, bring out his weaknesses."

"You should have gone to law school instead of flight school."

"Too much desk time. Seriously, you've got to go after this like you're in court." As comfortable in Brian's apartment as in his own, Mike snagged them each another beer.

"Corporate lawyers rarely go to court."

"They must have at least touched on it at Stanford," he returned, handing Brian a beer. "Prepare accordingly. This could be your second to last shot."

"Second to last?"

"Your last shot is being the ass in the back of the church." His eyes sparkled with challenge. "Thanks for the beer. I'll take this one to go."

"Where are you off to on a Sunday night? You're obviously not working."

"Nope. I have a date." He tossed Brian a parting glance over his shoulder. "I'm still waiting for that look…in the mirror."

Nodding to Mike's retreating back, Brian polished off his beer, then cracked open the second. Walking out on the balcony, he inhaled the cool, damp air as his eyes swept the city humming below. The fog washed over the skyline like a sea of cotton, but for Salesforce Tower lighting up the city like a beacon in the night. He tried to remember the last time he'd come out here and enjoyed the view for which he paid so dearly. Before Lindsay left, no doubt.

The ring of his cell phone interrupted his thoughts and the sound of his daughter's voice instantly lifted his spirits. "Hey, Dad."

"Hey, Kelse."

"Sorry I missed your call earlier. We can't have our phones in the guard chair."

"No problem. How was the beach today?"

"Hot and crowded. I'm tired."

"Me too. Are we still on for the weekend after next?"

"Yeah. Mom and I are going school shopping next weekend."

"School shopping?"

"You know, clothes, stuff for my dorm room, supplies."

"We can do that here, too. Save a few things for me to buy."

"Mom says you buy plenty. Much more than you should."

"Kelse, what else would I do with my money but spend it on you?"

"I don't know," his daughter replied rhetorically. "Do something for yourself. I wish you had someone else to spend it on. I hate that you're alone when I'm not there. Mom worries about you too."

"Tell Mom not to worry." Brian swallowed an unexpected tug of emotion. "Actually, I'll tell her myself." He wanted to split whatever Laura spent on Kelsey this weekend down the middle. "Is she home?"

"No. She and Tom went out for their anniversary. I'm babysitting."

"I'll catch-up with her later then." He paused, then asked, "How many years is it for them now?"

"Ten."

He and Laura had barely made it half that far. "Wow."

"I know. I hardly remember life without him."

Brian bit back the sting. But Tom had been good to Kelsey, which went a long way in his book. He cleared his throat and changed the subject. "How's the car running?"

"The way a brand new convertible should. Thank you again."

"You're more than welcome. Well-deserved, graduating magna cum laude from one of the top ranked high schools in the country."

"Still...Oh, can you hold on? That's Mom."

"I'll let you go. Love you, Kelse."

"Love you, Dad."

Brian reveled in her words for a few seconds after the beep of disconnection and then leaned over the balcony, taking in the city with a thoughtful sip. He couldn't believe Laura had been remarried for a decade. If he'd met Lindsay ten years ago, would he have done the same? Hardly, he snorted, straightening up. She would have been practically Kelsey's age now.

He hadn't set out to be alone, it had just happened. He'd dated some, but Lindsay had been his first real relationship since his marriage. She'd filled a void in his life he hadn't known existed. Until it was empty again, like it was now. And as brakes squeaked and foghorns bellowed around him, sudden panic rose inside him. Because if he lost her again, it might be that way forever.

She'd said she had to leave to survive. Is that what he'd been doing this past year? These past fifteen years? Merely surviving? Living and surviving, Brian realized as he walked inside, are two very different things. He finished the beer and threw the bottle into the recycling bin. Hard enough to shatter it into a million tiny pieces, as if it had never been whole.

CHAPTER SEVEN

LINDSAY GRIMACED AT THE cool spray hitting her face as the boat pressed on. They hadn't made plans for today, so when Paul appeared on her dock with a rented ski boat and a picnic lunch, she was surprised to say the least. And strangely relieved. Because she'd spent the twenty-four hours since Brian left debating both his impetuous offer and her portentous conversation with Moira. Fate might be her friend after all. And now it seemed to have partnered with that little voice inside her head. She studied her fiancé at the helm with new resolve, likening him to a long-coveted Christmas present. Wished for the first year your head knows there's not a Santa Claus, but your heart still pretends. Then you come downstairs on Christmas morning and find everything you wanted in one beautifully wrapped package. But you open it to find that one of the pieces is missing. Yet you keep it because it still works. Most of the time.

The shoreline whizzed by as Paul sprinted over the waves, heading for Sand Harbor. Lindsay was surprised when he killed the engine just short of the beach on the lake's rocky eastern shore. She gave him a curious look and replaced her sun hat. "We're stopping here?"

"Just for a minute. I want to run something by you," Paul began, retrieving the anchor from one of the bolsters lining the starboard side of the boat. "If we're going to have the ceremony on the beach, mid-October is as far out as we can safely go weather-wise. And since it's the shoulder season, we'll have no trouble finding a caterer, photographer and the like," he went on enthusiastically. "Even on short notice."

Like three months. "Okay," Lindsay replied, joining him at the bow.

"So I was thinking— I swear you can see fifty feet down today," Paul interrupted himself, monitoring the anchor's progress. "If it's this clear here, Sand Harbor will be lucid to seventy."

"Or more. You know better than anyone how insidious the lake can be."

Paul's jaw tightened. "That was years ago."

"It doesn't change what you did. You saved Jack's life that day."

"And I'll never let him forget it. All because Michelle wanted a pretty rock." Rolling his eyes, he brought Lindsay to him. "Speaking of rocks, we still need to have yours sized. But that's not why I took the day off." Placing his hands on her shoulders, he angled her toward the shore. "How would you feel about having the reception at Thunderbird Lodge?"

Lindsay rested her gaze on the old Tudor mansion holding court on the edge of a rugged cliff. Nestled by towering conifers and granite boulders, it was the epitome of Lake Tahoe with its subtle grandeur and bulky stone architecture. She shrugged, indifferent. "I've passed it a million times, but never thought to go inside. There's some crazy legend about the man who built it."

"More truth than legend. It was built by an eccentric millionaire from San Francisco. There are tall tales about all-night poker games and wild parties in the '30s and '40s. Movie stars, railroad magnates, a veritable zoo of wild animals. It's a museum of sorts now, and available to rent for special occasions. We could still get married on your beach, then shuttle the guests over here," he explained with cautious hope shining in his eyes. "What do you think?"

Her eyes cut back to the iconic mansion. She visualized herself in her mother's dress, walking down the stone staircase on Mr. Brody's arm. Dancing with Paul as soft music drifted through the lush gardens and into the dense forestland beyond. Guests mingling about as the lake went to sleep to a lullaby of crashing waves. Turning back to him, she wrapped her arms around his waist, and bringing them both under the brim of her hat, pressed her lips to his. "I think it's a great idea."

"You do, huh?" he gushed, lust leaping into his eyes. The hem of her dress rose just above the cuff of his shorts and their bare thighs touched. "Linds...." he muttered, holding her face in the palms of his hands and drawing her into a possessive kiss.

Her stomach flipped, but her heartbeat remained steady. Even as he roamed her torso with his fingertips, it didn't jump. Her breath caught a bit when he cupped her breasts, but her nipples remained flaccid. Still she accepted, reciprocated, contended, as he grew against her. The way, she recalled regretfully, Brian had yesterday.

"That's the Lindsay I'm marrying, the Lindsay I've missed," Paul admitted with bated breath, resting his forehead against hers. "The Lindsay I can't wait to make love to."

She tried to hide the misgiving rolling through her. Swallowing hard, she pulled back. "Missed?"

"You've been so distracted, so distant lately. I was getting a little concerned." His voice trailed off. "Now it sounds silly, but I was afraid you were having second thoughts." He gave her a tight-lipped grin and laughed without opening his mouth. "I even said something to Moira the other day."

"Really?" Lindsay mocked astonishment.

Paul shot her a clever look. "As if you didn't know. She assured me everything is fine." His brow furrowed. "Everything is fine, right?"

Not quite yet, but it would be. She would see to it. "Yes, of course. Why wouldn't it be?"

*****

"Have you eaten today?" Jan Carpenter followed Brian into his office.

"Not that I remember."

"That's what I thought," she replied, pulling a sandwich and a banana out of thin air. Placing it on Brian's desk, she grabbed a bottle of water from the compact refrigerator in the corner, ordering, "Sit and eat."

Brian obliged, knowing he didn't have a choice.

"Busy morning?" Jan sat in one of the arm chairs opposite his desk and looked at him expectantly.

"You could say that," he managed in between bites.

"Looks like you had a busy weekend as well."

"I took an impromptu trip if that's what you mean."

"You know that's not what I mean."

Brian stopped chewing. "Is anything sacred?"

"Of course not." Jan leaned forward, eyes gleaming. "The florist called to say the roses won't be delivered until tomorrow or Wednesday. The shipment that arrived this morning was not up to your usual standards." Her face lit up like a Christmas tree. "So, you're seeing Lindsay again?"

"I'm working on it. I ran into her in Tahoe, asked her to visit next weekend." Brian took a long draw of water. "Anything pressing we need to deal with?"

She ignored his attempt to change the subject. "Can I make you a dinner reservation somewhere?

How about Scoma's? It's her favorite if I remember correctly."

"No. And yes, you do," Brian answered shortly, glancing at the stack of messages in front of him. "I didn't say she was coming."

"Why wouldn't she be coming?"

Brain let out a long, slow sigh. He wasn't going to get out of this so easily. "Because, Jan, Lindsay is getting married."

"Married?" Jan didn't try to hide her shock.

"Yes, it came as quite a surprise to me as well."

"So you didn't straighten out whatever happened between you two?"

"No. If we had she wouldn't be getting married, would she?"

"I suppose not. In that case, what's your plan?"

Why was everyone asking him that? "I don't have a plan. I don't even have an answer. There's no sense in—"

"If she wasn't at least considering it, she would have already declined," Jan cut him off. She stood and began pacing, index finger over her mouth and thumb below her chin. Her platinum bob shined in the afternoon sunlight and her eyes were serious, thoughtful, crafty. Brian could all but see the wheels turning in her head. "You'll have to make the next few days count," she connived. "The flowers are a good start. But you've got to exploit the other guy's weak spot. Something's missing or she would have refused right off the bat." She stopped and met Brian's gaze. "What do you know about him?"

"Jan, this is ludicrous."

"No, counselor," she corrected firmly, "it's discovery."

"Speaking of discovery, I need to get back to work." He began thumbing through the pink slips of paper arranged neatly on his desk.

His assistant walked over to the desk, leaned forward and quieted his hands with hers. "There's nothing here that can't wait."

Brian returned the look of warmhearted irritation. "Jan, please. I don't want to talk about this right now."

"Fine. I'll do the talking," she said, straightening up. "Do you know why I never remarried?"

Tossing the papers aside in surrender, Brian answered, "No."

"Because my husband was the love of my life. I thought I had it all—great kids, strong marriage, house in the suburbs." Jan walked to the window and stared at the crystal blue sky. "Then one day a woman called the house asking for Joe. He was out; it was his poker night. I ignored my intuition that time. Several weeks later one of the men Joe played cards with called looking for him. I was beside myself, thinking he'd gotten in an accident or something. Of course that was long before cell phones," she reminded him. "I drove around frantically looking for him. Where do you think I found him?"

Brian huffed out a breath. "I don't know."

"In a restaurant in downtown Pleasanton. With a lovely young woman. I'll never forget the look on his face when he saw me through the window." She pivoted on the fog-colored carpeting with distant eyes. "Poker night went from weekly to biweekly. He'd gotten his weeks mixed-up."

Why was she baring her soul now, after all these years? "Jan, I'm sorry. You don't need to tell me all of this."

"I do, actually. You'll see why in a minute. I asked him to leave that night. Joe begged me to forgive him; she meant nothing to him. It had just happened. He promised never to see her again. But there was no gray area for me." Her voice cracked. "We were divorced within the year."

"Jan, please, don't upset yourself."

"He did everything imaginable to get me back," she continued, undaunted. "Every time he picked up the boys, he brought something for me. Even a fur coat on my birthday one year. I refused it, of course." She leaned in close to Brian. "Do you know what the biggest regret of my life is?"

Knowing she didn't expect an answer, Brian stared into her hazy gray eyes and shook his head from side to side.

"That I didn't give him another chance. I never felt anything close to how I felt about Joe again. I think it was the same for him," she conceded. "Because of my stubbornness, neither one of us was ever truly happy again." She laid her hands on Brian's shoulders. "It's too late for us. But you have been given a second chance. Take it. Before it's too late. No one deserves it more than you." She gave him a half-hearted smile and walked out, shutting the door behind her.

Leaning back in his chair, Brian sent a meditative stare out the window at the Bay Bridge. It was already jammed with commuters leaving the city. Going home to families, home-cooked meals, soccer games. But not him. He would work late tonight and if he thought of it, eat whatever Jan had ordered him for dinner. After a few weighty beats, Brian's attention returned to his desk and the matters at hand. Deep in work mode, he didn't realize how much time had passed until the phone rang.

"Perbacco tonight, huh Mr. Rembrandt?" said the gruff voice on the other end of the line. "Better get down here on the double. Smells mighty good. Lasagna, I'm guessing. Can't be responsible for my actions much longer."

Brian carved out a smile. "You know what, Ken, it's yours," he told the night guard. "I had a late lunch."

"Oh no, sir. I couldn't," he replied with borrowed conviction.

Brian laughed under his breath, imagining the old-timer popping up in his chair. "Well, you'd better. Jan would have a fit if it went to waste. What's the score of the Giants game, by the way?" Brian asked, settling the matter. "Chicago's in town, right?"

"We're up two to nothing, bottom of the fifth."

"Very good. Let me know if we pull it out."

"You'll be here for a while then, sir."

"Yeah," Brian answered, watching the head-lights inch across the bridge. "I'll be here for a while."

CHAPTER EIGHT

LINDSAY THREW HER KEYS on the kitchen counter and flipped through the mail, humming to herself. They'd found the most beautiful lot. The house would be perched in the foothills of Mt. Rose with sweeping views of the Sierras, the Reno skyline and the valley. The foreground of the property was sagebrush and stone, but the back of the lot would be leveled for sod and flower gardens.

The flashing red light on the phone beckoned her and hitting the play button, she began sorting the junk from the pertinent mail. She was silently praising herself for not thinking about Brian all afternoon when his voice filled the room. "Hey, Linds, give me a call back. I couldn't get through on your cell." She froze in place as her heart began to race and her stomach fell while the answering machine beeped again and played on. "This is Andy from Flowers and Such calling for Ms. Foster. We've missed you twice and the customer is none too happy, wants this delivery made tonight. We'll try again on our way back to the shop." She was still standing there in awe when a knock sounded on the door. Pushing away the idea the two messages were related, she answered it. "Yes?"

A young man wearing a baseball cap and a relieved smile greeted her on the other side. "Ms. Foster?"

"I'm Lindsay Foster."

"Great. I trust you got my message." He pointed to the depiction of a chrysanthemum on his hat. "Where do you want 'em all?"

"Them all?"

"Yeah. There are sixteen bouquets. All white roses."

"*Sixteen?*" Lindsay amazed. "Oh, umm...I guess on the dining room table," she directed on the fly.

"Will do," he agreed, eyeing the round table over Lindsay's shoulder. "But that isn't going to hold all of them. We'll have to split them up," he suggested amenably, heading for a white van parked in the driveway.

"The kitchen island, then, I guess," she conjectured to his retreating back.

He waved in acknowledgement, then slid the van door open. He returned presently with an arrangement in each hand. "Anniversary, ma'am?"

"What? Oh, no."

"Sixteenth Birthday?" He winked conspiringly.

"Hardly. But thanks anyway."

"None of my business, of course. But such a unique order usually signifies something, like a birthday or anniversary." He put the flowers down on the table and started to retrace his steps until something caught his eye, stopping him short. "Wow."

Now what? Bears had been active this year, but she'd secured the garbage this morning.

"What a view," Andy finished, interrupting her thoughts. "I've lived here all my life and that's one of the best views of the lake I've ever seen."

Lindsay relaxed. "Thanks, but the hotel down the beach gives mine a run for its money." She paused, then feeling compelled to explain said, "This was my grandparents' house."

The Weatheralls, right?"

"That's right."

"My grandfather started our shop around the same time yours opened the first supermarket in town if I understand correctly."

"Yes, after the War, I think."

"Seemed to work out a little better for you, though. I'm still living at home. My dad is making me start at the bottom."

Apparently Andy had missed a few pages in her family storybook. He still had a father. "My grandfather sold the business long ago, so working it wasn't in the cards for me. You'll thank your dad in the end. You'll know the business from the ground up."

"I suppose," Andy conceded with a reluctant shrug and went back out to the truck.

Shaking her head in disbelief, Lindsay watched him bring in the next batch. "It's unlike my fiancé to be so extravagant."

"Sixteen days 'til the wedding maybe? Getting married on the sixteenth of the month?"

"Neither."

"Well, I'm sure you'll figure it out. It's the thought that counts anyway," he threw over his shoulder, picking up the pace a bit.

She walked over to the table and plucked a stem, wincing at the thorny petiole. Maybe that's what makes a rose so special. You have to fight past the thorns to earn the velvety petals above. She held the bud to her nose and inhaled, shutting her eyes as her mouth automatically curved.

"Well, that's the last of 'em."

Replacing the flower, she grabbed her wallet and met him at the door. "Thank you for coming back."

"No problem. And the tip has been taken care of as well," he told her, waving away the bills. "I just need a signature." He handed her an iPad and after she obliged, traded it for a small envelope. "Nice talking to you." He wished her good night and left.

The sweet scent of violet and balsam filled the room as she opened the envelope and retrieved the tiny card inside. "Huh," she grunted to herself. It wasn't Paul's handwriting, but a woman's. Odd that he would have called in the order.

Then she realized he didn't.

She should have known. Her hands began to shake as she reread the sinuous script. *White roses signify a new beginning. Start ours on Friday. Love, Brian.* Feeling her eyes well with tears, she lowered herself to the arm of the couch and unfolded the enclosed piece of paper. Her heart leapt into her throat when she realized it was a flight itinerary.

She hadn't shared Brian's invitation with anyone, even Moira. And as Monday turned into Tuesday and Tuesday into today, she told herself that was for the best. He'd asked her in the heat of the moment, and she'd agreed to consider it in the heat of that same passionate moment. But that moment was gone. He'd gone back to his life in San Francisco and she had bought a lot and sized her ring. By the time Brian came up for air from the All Tech case she'd likely be married. Lindsay walked out on the deck and dropped wearily into a chair, watching the silver-tipped waves crash unyieldingly against the shore in the alpenglow. Damn Brian anyway. He'd finally come for her. Sixteen months too late.

CHAPTER NINE

"TELL ME WHY WE'RE here again?" Brian asked Mike.

"Because I'm starving and you haven't seen the light of day since Monday. Sunday for all I know. You might have gone in before dawn."

"And we had to come here?"

"We didn't have too. We could have gone to the Castro or the Tenderloin. But since it's just the two of us…"

Brian met Mike's knowing look with an equitable smirk. "Very funny."

"Come on, where else can you find barking sea lions, bread dough being twisted into any shape imaginable and a wax museum all in one place?"

"Don't forget the hordes of people waiting to use the bathroom at McDonald's and the guy selling sweatshirts for a borderline criminal price," Brian countered, loosening his tie.

"God, you really do hate the Wharf don't you?"

"I don't hate the Wharf. I hate what it has become. A tourist trap. When I first came to Stanford, it was different. Busy, noisy, alive; not shamelessly commercialized. Laura and I used to come here just to people-watch. It was free entertainment for broke college students."

"There's also fresh seafood, awesome views and," Mike threw a few bills into the weathered guitar case of a street musician, "great music."

Brian began with a sigh. "You're right. I've grown cynical over the years."

"Especially this last one." Mike paused, then decided to go on. "Any word from Lindsay?"

"No," Brian replied as they approached the cable car turnaround. Other than being in his every thought, his every breath, he inwardly grumbled.

"She got the flowers?"

"Last night. Jan got a signature confirmation."

"And she didn't call? To thank you?"

"Nope."

"Harsh. What now?"

"We came down here to eat, right?"

Mike matched Brian's edgy tone. "I mean about Lindsay, not dinner."

"I guess I got my answer. Where to?"

"Since I'll be in Rome tomorrow, anything but Italian. How about Scoma's?"

"Sure," Brian replied flippantly. "I haven't been there in a while."

"Me neither. I've been in the air more than I've been home."

They turned on Powell and after a few moments of companionable silence, Mike said, "That doesn't sound like her. Not to call, I mean."

No, it didn't. "Maybe she didn't like them."

"What woman doesn't like 192 roses?"

"A stubborn one."

"Or a scared one."

Brian stopped walking. "What does *she* have to be afraid of?"

"Let's see." Mike cocked his head to the side and began wryly. "An old boyfriend appears out of the woodwork, casting a shadow of doubt over the silver platter on which Mr. Perfect has served her the world. There's unresolved business with the former, but all things considered, it's more prudent to go the safe route, stick with the sure thing. Secretly she considers the invitation, though, before compartmentalizing it and tucking it away. Far, far away where no one else goes. Except for the ghost of you, that is. Then, in a move characteristic of said old boyfriend, a bouquet of flowers for every month they've been apart arrives, sporting an airline ticket. First class, knowing you, which is a bit of a waste for such a short flight, but sends a worthy message."

Brian's chest tightened. Is that all he was? An old boyfriend?

Mike started walking again without missing a beat. "This throws her into an emotional frenzy, resulting in further internal debate that she has accepted Superman's proposal prematurely. But Lindsay's pragmatic mind wins out over her wavering heart. She isn't the kind of woman to spend the weekend with one man and go home to another, so accepting your invitation would mean telling Mr.

High School about her doubts and wine-fueled indiscretion. Which jeopardizes her future and evades all common sense."

"You've given this a freakish amount of thought."

With a look of mocked annoyance, Mike barreled on. "Still, she's left with the matter of the flowers. If she calls to thank you, you'll ask about the weekend and she'll have to say no, of course. She's damned if she does and damned if she doesn't because part of her wants to go, and the other part knows she can't. And being the accomplished attorney that you are, she can expect an exhausting argument that will only twist the knots in her stomach tighter. So she'll decide it's best to leave a message."

The crowds were growing thicker as they approached Jefferson Street, their chin music blending with the sound of foghorns cutting through the soupy air. All Brian could say was, "Okay."

"She'll consider calling in the wee hours of the night; she's been up all week anyway. But since you practically sleep with your phone under your pillow, she can't chance it," Mike speculated zealously. "There's always the office, banking on a time when you've given Jan implicit instructions not to be interrupted, of which there's a possibility with your current workload." Mike shook away the possibility with a tight-lipped grin. "But that's risky. Lindsay knows Jan has a soft spot for her, and might patch her through anyway. She could ask me to pass along the gratitude, but there's always a chance of us being together. Especially since the Giants are above 500 this season and I have box seats," Mike paused, his eyes shining with good humor.

Brian reeled in his jaw. "You're unbelievable. If I didn't know better, I'd swear you'd been a woman in another life."

Mike held up a hand and collapsed his thumb into his palm. "Four older sisters, remember?"

"So, in your professional opinion, Dr. Savoy, what will she do?"

"One of two things. Wait until the weekend window has passed and then call to thank you for the flowers."

"Or?" Brian wanted to know.

"She accepted the delivery, so there's still a chance she'll come." Mike leaned against a pier stump, joined his legs at the ankles and crossed his arms. "But I don't think that's going to happen. So, you really have no other choice."

"Yeah, you're right. She's right." Brian sounded more convinced than he felt inside. Shoving his hands in his pockets, he hung his head and kicked the ground. "We're the same people we were last year. Why set ourselves up to get hurt again?"

Mike shot Brian a pitiful look. "You know, for a smart guy you sure are dumb sometimes. She had that look in her eyes too, you idiot. You gotta go get her."

CHAPTER TEN

"SO DO YOU THINK he'll go for it? Or should I be asking you since you actually run the place?"

"As if my father doesn't already consider you his second daughter, your fiancé saved my brother's life. So you can pretty much write your own ticket around here," Moira replied from her desk.

Lindsay ran a finger across the desk in the corner, loaded with yellowed papers and dusty files. It came up white. Fanning a hand in front of her face she feigned coughing, saying, "I don't need much. Just a small work area and permission to solicit your clients. Maybe peek into your book of business for leads."

"That's fine," Moira muttered, eyes glued to the computer screen. "Dad would rather give you the business than the highbrow interior designer we refer clients to now."

"You won't even know I'm here," Lindsay promised.

"Even better," Moira teased without looking up. "But don't you need a license or something?"

"Not until I start charging. I'm just testing the waters for now."

"You should take some pictures of your place. Make a portfolio."

"I'm a step ahead of you. Took some shots this morning," Lindsay informed her, reaching into her bag and retrieving her DSLR camera. She sauntered over to Moira's beyond cluttered desk. "Wanna see?"

"Yeah. In a sec." She gave the keyboard a few pecks. "There. Done." She leaned forward and met Lindsay's gaze with an expectant smile. "Dazzle me."

Lindsay watched her friend scan through the pictures. She wore jeans and a T-shirt, in typical contrast to the silk skirt and embellished tank top Lindsay had selected. Moira had such understated, natural beauty, with her ringlet curls framing her china doll face. The freckles dotting her nose reminded Lindsay of the countless summer days they'd spent at the lake, burying each other in the sand, sharing secrets, becoming the sister neither one of them had.

"These are great, but there's hardly any of the downstairs," Moira commented, interrupting Lindsay's thoughts. "Especially the kitchen. And take a wider shot of the living and dining rooms together. Highlight that table you had made in Italy. It's the focal part of the room."

Moira was right, of course. But the handcrafted table was bursting with flowers. "I will. I wanted to run my idea by you first."

"And why is this flower arrangement in every shot?" Moira asked, turning the screen toward Lindsay. "The white roses are a nice contrast to your dark woods, but they don't pop. I'm surprised you chose them. They're a little traditional for your taste."

Their eyes held for a few seconds. Then, standing slowly, Moira realized out loud, "You didn't choose them, did you?" Her head snapped back to the camera and she began studying the images more purposefully. "Lovers send red, friends yellow. White roses fall somewhere in between." She swallowed hard and met Lindsay's gaze. "Brian sent these, didn't he?"

Damn Moira anyway. She was too smart for her own good. Not that she wouldn't have told her eventually. With an affirming nod, Lindsay spat out, "He asked me to come to San Francisco this weekend. Sent me a ticket. It arrived last night along with sixteen dozen roses."

Surprise tumbled across Moira's face instead of the shock Lindsay had expected. She raised her eyebrows and nodded. "Clever. Go on."

"He was waiting for me when I got home from the wedding on Saturday night. Ambushed me at the door. I had been drinking," Lindsay elaborated, crossing the room and wringing her hands. "He kissed me. I responded...elementally, let's say. The next morning—"

"He stayed the night?"

"On the couch. Nothing happened," Lindsay quickly clarified. "Things got a little hot and heavy the next day, though."

"Was that before or after he asked you to visit?" Moira called her out.

Lindsay matched her supposed stare directly. "Before."

"I assume you're not going. Seeing how you've set a wedding date and booked a reception venue."

"No, I'm not going."

"Did you tell him why?"

"Yeah. That's when he invited me to San Francisco."

Moira rolled her eyes, then squinted in annoyed confusion. "So you refused before he asked?"

"No, he asked me to visit after I told him I was getting married," she explained with a shrug. "It's his competitive nature."

"So, let me get this straight," Moira began, stepping out from behind the desk. "Brian appears at your door. You get a little ahead of yourselves. You attempt to resolve the situation by informing him that you're getting married. Despite that, he asks you to visit him."

Close enough. "Not to stay at his place," Lindsay added hurriedly. "He offered me a room at the Fairmont."

"Forever the gentleman," Moira muttered. "Then what? You declined? End of story?"

"He guilted me into agreeing to consider it. Said I owed him that."

"He's right. You do."

Whose side was Moira on anyway? Lindsay ignored her words, but banked her strained expression. "Who does Brian think he is?" She waved an indignant hand in the air. "Waltzing in here after all this time, expecting me to drop my life for him." She finished with her hands on her hips.

"Did he ask you not to get married?"

"No," Lindsay answered quietly, lowering her eyes. "But he asked me why I was getting married."

"What did you tell him?"

"The truth. I love Paul. I'd be a fool not to marry him."

"So how did you leave it with him?" Moira asked after a long moment of silence.

"I haven't spoken to him since he left on Sunday."

"No wonder you look so tired. Bet you haven't slept all week."

"I was up half the night debating how to acknowledge the delivery and thank him without having to speak with him directly." She returned to Moira and went on, increasingly encouraged as her plan became tangible. "So I'm going to call his cell later this afternoon. Providing the partners' meeting is still on Thursdays, he won't pick up. I'll cancel the ticket with the airline and have his account credited."

Moira nodded agreeably. "Did you tell Paul?"

"I thought about it. But it would only hurt him and wouldn't change anything." Lindsay's voice dropped off. "I feel bad enough as it is."

With a sympathetic grin, Moira took her into a warm embrace. "I know."

"You know me better than anyone. I'm doing the right thing, aren't I?" she impressed upon Moira as the half-hearted relief of coming clean to her washed some of the guilt away.

"I can't tell you that," Moira replied as they broke apart. "You have to listen to your heart."

That was easier said than done. Because the little voice inside Lindsay's head was saying something completely different.

CHAPTER ELEVEN

THE CLICK OF THE camera broke through the still air. The lull before the storm, Lindsay thought, raising her eyes to the darkening sky. Of course the logical thing to do would be to stage the inside and get those photos done while the storm passed over. But that was impossible. She had to stay out of the house. She'd had the sense to keep the roses out of her bedroom, but their scent still filled every nook of cranny of the place. She'd considered giving them to a nursing home or hospital, but couldn't bring herself to do it. Paul, being out of town for a few days, had granted her that indulgence.

The seminal impatiens were filling in nicely, bordered by flowering salvia in the back and the flagstone bricks in the front. With love and luck, they would spread and swell, shrouding the stacked stones in bushels of color. But that would take weeks, she reminded herself, crouching down for a close-up shot. And she wanted to print these pictures today. Putting together the portfolio would occupy her mind through the weekend. Scrunching her shoulders, Lindsay rubbed away the goose bumps erupting on her arms and walked around to the front of the house. Thunderheads towered over the mountains like an eerie black dome, dropping a curtain of rain on the eastern shore. The weather was coming in fast. A few curb shots and she would be forced to call it a day, she decided with a sudden shiver. By the time she was done, the wind was howling fiercely and the sky's ceiling had fallen along with the temperature. But that's not why a chill trickled down her spine. It was the reproachful voice behind her.

"You missed your flight."

Her hand froze on the door handle and after counting to five to collect herself, she replied, "I left you a message."

The hand attached to the voice gripped her arm and swung her around. "Your message thanked me for the flowers. It said nothing about the flight. Or the weekend."

The steel blue eyes staring back at her were as merciless as the choppy gray peaks pummeling the shore. Lindsay swallowed the lump in her throat and managed, "I thought you understood. I couldn't come."

"You said you'd think about it."

"And I did," she maintained, lifting her chin. "I decided it wasn't a good idea."

"I disagree." Brian braced his hands on the door jam, trapping her between his arms, and spoke in a low growl. "Do you know how hard it was for me to get a flight to Reno on a Friday afternoon in July?"

She sucked a breath. "No."

"I had to buy my way on or wait until morning. Luckily, I found an entrepreneurial college kid who likes to drive." Hedging her in, he paused for a moment and then asked, "Do you know why I did that?"

Knowing he didn't expect an answer, Lindsay merely gulped.

"Because I was already at the airport," he continued with thready breaths. "And," he slanted his mouth over hers, "I couldn't wait until tomorrow to do this." Brian crushed his mouth on hers. It was white-hot. Burning as intensely as the fire he'd stirred within her. Resisting glimmered, dulled, then dissipated in her mind. Instead her arms linked his neck and she melted into the heat. He tasted rugged, felt rough, like the end of a long day. Their mouths collided, parted, rejoined, until they found that familiar crescendo and began the climb. The flame caught, flickered, combusted, as Brian's tongue tangled with hers and his hands combed her back. And then a flare began to kindle in another place, deep within her. Even through the denim, Brian was rising to meet it, fill it. Rigid against her, he released her mouth and buried his face in her hair. "When I told you I wasn't giving up so easily this time, I meant it." He stepped out of her embrace and taking her hands in his, asked, "Should I leave?"

His eyes had softened to make room for his heart, she realized. And she could deny hers no longer. Thoroughly disarmed, she could only shake her head from side to side.

The corners of Brian's mouth curved, but his expression remained tight. "Then we need to get something straight. If I come in, I'm going to stay," he informed her in a disturbingly reasonable tone of voice. "And if I stay, I'm going to make love to you all night long."

She should tell him to go. Ignore the ripples in her stomach, the way her heart was chasing them. Instead she heard herself surrender to them. "Promise?"

He pushed away the windblown tendrils that had fallen into her face. "Promise."

Pine cones screeched across the asphalt and spring's forgotten leaves danced on the grass in the rising wind as he opened the front door and led her up the stairs. No words were necessary; he knew the way. To her bed, to her heart, to her soul. Telling rain began beating against the roof as he laid her on the bed. Laying next to her, he swept his fingertips across her lips. "I've never wanted anyone the way I want you, Lindsay," he told her with a kiss. "Even you."

Pulse leaping to join his, she ordered in a husky voice, "Show me."

They exchanged a look of poignant understanding. Then Brian rolled on top of her, seamlessly moving his body onto hers. Ranging himself between her legs, he framed her face with his arms and in a voice as thick as honey, confided, "I haven't been with anybody else."

Lindsay was dumbfounded. "You haven't?"

"No."

"Neither have I."

That seemed to shock, then please him. Immensely. "But what about…" he faltered.

She shook her head from side to side, noting the hint of prayer in his voice. "You were the last man to touch me," she told him, throat swelling.

The weight of her words filled his lustful eyes with delight and appreciation. "I've waited sixteen months to make love to you again. I can't wait much longer."

She lifted her arms to circle his neck and skimmed her lips across his. "Who's asking you to?"

The challenge registered in his eyes as his mouth took hers. He set his sights on her bottom lip and pulled, as if to tease, before covering her mouth with his. He let the kiss simmer a bit, sink in, layer by feverish layer. Then came his tongue. It began a slow meander down her throat and décolletage while his thumbs traced the thin cotton of her shirt until her nipples, now turgid, stood on point. Finally he slipped the shirt over her head, jettisoning it to the floor before making quick work of her bra. She'd laid in bed many a night dreaming about this. Remembering the way her head bowed back as Brian caressed her breasts. The way her gut coiled into a spool of desire when his tongue drew a tortuously slow line down her torso to her belly button and back to her mouth again. The way the swooning in her head became a creamy deluge between her thighs.

He allowed himself a few seconds to wallow in her heaving breasts. "You are so beautiful. How have I gone this long without you?"

Lindsay could ask herself the same question. She could already feel the orgasm starting to build inside of her. Bringing his face back up to hers by way of reply, she commandeered his mouth, then his tongue as he reacquainted himself with her curves. Finally coming up for air, she could wait no more. "Brian, now."

He inched her jeans down. Holding their weighted stare, he knelt above her, unbuttoning his shirt from the top as she worked it from the bottom. When their hands met, he stilled hers on this cock. "Oh," she growled. He was as hard as she was wet. Unbuckling his belt, he kicked off his jeans. He slid her panties, all that separated them now, over her hips and crawled back to her. His burgeoning erection nudged at her as he cupped her and every cell in her body went on high alert in anticipation of him. She spread her legs in whole-hearted invitation, whimpering when he found her creases. His fingers knew each tuck, each fold, each pleat of her. His thumb settled on the fleshy part of her core and began to stroke. She trembled, purred, pleaded, until finally he plunged into her seeping center. His fingers thrust in and out as she rocked beneath him, digging her nails into his back as her sharp, short gasps of pleasure filled the air. But that was nothing compared to the drone that escaped Brian's throat when he entered her. She tightened around him, dripping as he grew inside her, grinding against him as he rode her. She lifted her buttocks and brought him deeper still, raising her hips to increase the friction, pushing him farther into her as his abdomen sailed over hers. The spasms built, retreated, then roared back in full force as the tip of him pounded the most remote part of her. The climax ripped through her with such wielding power that she howled once, then again and begged for more. And just before Brian filled her, he obliged.

*****

They lay wrapped in each other on the rumpled comforter as the shadows grew long and the breeze stirred the Aspens. Brian skated a finger across Lindsay's forearm and even though he'd just had her, could think of nothing else but having her again. For a much longer session this time. "I loved making love with you," he told her, tightening his grip.

"I loved making love with you, too," she echoed into the crook of his shoulder.

"I want to do it again." He stroked that spot just above her tailbone, and felt her heart begin to canter. And himself begin to grow. "And again after that."

She twirled the lone corkscrew of hair on the center of his chest around her finger. "You did promise," she reminded him. "Something about all night long."

"I plan to make love to you for a lot longer than that."

At that, she reared her head and studied his face before stroking his cheek with the back of her hand. Then she kissed him long and hard. "Let's concentrate on tonight."

His brain wanted to debate the sudden change in her demeanor, but he was too mesmerized by her hand roaming slowly down his torso to put forth the effort. He took note of the hollowness in her eyes, but her hand wrapping around his cock took that notion to task. He tried to scoot closer, but her thumb rubbing the tip of his erection proved too distracting. "Baby, slow down," he half-heartedly panted, reaching for her hand.

She shot him a coy smile. "You don't like it?"

"No, I love it." He bit back the need. "But I don't want to come without you"

"Don't worry, I won't let you."

Brian begged to differ. He was already oozing readiness, swelling at a precarious rate and throbbing with all the brute force his collective blood flow had to offer. He had imminent visions of flipping Lindsay over like a pancake and burying himself inside her. "It might not be up to either of us."

"I want to wait until you can't stand it. Until we both can't." With a wolfish grin, she grated against him. His mind went blank for the want, his cock was seeping and his eyes rolled back in his head. He could smell her sweltering desire, her ambrosial-like balminess, her pent-up need as she scraped her body over his.

Her taut nipples grazed his torso as she made her way down to his cock. Her slender fingers gripped, then steadied as she took hold of him in her mouth. She wrapped her lips around his shaft and began to suck. Brian's affirmations mingled with his hedonic moans as he buckled in her fast. Her fingers pumped where her lips clenched, consuming all of him and pushing him to the edge of reason. "Get up here now," he somehow managed. She released him and licking her way, mounted him. Brian muttered words of gratitude as she brought him into her and began to rock above him. He found her liquid marine eyes, amid the sea of disheveled, sexy hair flying madly around her. Trading her knees for the balls of her feet, she pressed on, ratcheting up the pace, maneuvering him within her to intensify the sweet agony. "Are you close? I can't hold on much long—" She cut him off with a low growl of pleasure before leaning back and constricting her thighs against his hips as he exploded into her. She fell against him, and as Brian gathered her back into his arms, he knew he could never live without her again.

CHAPTER TWELVE

BRIAN'S FEET HIT THE floor with a resounding thud and his heart followed suit when he saw Lindsay's disconsolate profile through the cracked deck door. She was pondering the day, knees to chest, hands entwined at the ankles. For a few moments only soft warbling and lazy undulations filled the air. Then as if clairvoyant, she turned to face him with a closemouthed smile. Jumping into his pants, he accepted her silent offer and joined her on the oversized deck chair. "Good Morning."

She leaned into him. "Good Morning."

"It would have been a great one if I hadn't woken up alone."

"Sorry. I couldn't get back to sleep."

Brian tightened his arm across her chest. "Who said anything about sleeping?"

"Bri, what happened last night…"

"Was incredible."

"Can never happen again." She looked up at him, her face etched in struggle, her eyes anguished. "Because I'm getting married," she finished with care.

The accordion in Brian's gut compressed as he bit back the shock. "The hell you are." Automatically stiffening, he let his arm fall away from her. "You don't marry one person when you're in love with someone else, sleeping with someone else."

She sprung to her feet. "We aren't—" She made air quotes with her fingers. "sleeping together. Last night was a lapse in judgment, a mistake made in the name of closure," she contended inadequately.

Brian's blood ran cold as the curl in his abdomen moved to his heart. He stood slowly and jabbing a finger in the air toward the bedroom, protested, "That was no mistake."

Her bottom lip began to quiver and burying her face in her hands, she began to sob.

That unnerved him, gave him two left feet as he went to her. "Linds—"

"No, don't. Just don't," she implored him, raising her palm in the air. "Whenever you come close to me, touch me, I melt."

A grin was threatening to sneak across his face, but Brian foiled it. "Then how can you go on pretending it's over between us?"

Tear tracks blistered her cheeks. "Because I have no other choice."

"The hell you don't," he fired back. "Break off the engagement. We can pick up where we left off."

Shaking her head, she walked to the deck railing. "No, Brian, we can't."

"I'm still in love with you, Linds," he heard himself say.

She threw her hands in the air, let them slap her thighs. "Oh, no! Don't say that. Don't you dare say that."

"It's true and mutual or last night wouldn't have happened." He raked his fingers through hair. "Especially the second round."

That seemed to stun, then oddly settle her. Her eyes narrowed and her teeth clenched, stretching her full lips into a tight line. "That was low. You know you're the only man I've..." She pressed her hand to her mouth as her voice trailed off.

"Precisely. So you must still love me or you wouldn't have done it," he countered, going to her. "It was mind-boggling, by the way. You haven't lost your touch."

She pushed at him. "I can't do this. I can't fall in love with you again."

"Too late."

"Brian!" Her eyes widened as she over-enunciated. "I'm getting married." She sighed and looked away. "I guess I wanted to remember what it felt like to be with you, to bond with you, one more time."

"Bullshit. It's more than that and you know it. You take sex too seriously to just—" He stopped short, feeling pounds lighter as the revelation sunk in. "That's why you haven't slept with Webster, isn't it? Because you don't really love him."

Lindsay didn't dispute him, just stared at the water unseeingly.

Increasingly encouraged, he trudged on. "So it's a marriage of convenience. On your part, anyway."

Her gaze snapped back to him and squaring her shoulders, she told him, "It is not. It's much more than that. Sex doesn't define a relationship or even a marriage. What Paul and I have is much deeper than that."

"It couldn't be any deeper than last night. Or this morning." He paused, reloaded, as the up-turn of his lips spread to his eyes. "But I guess you wouldn't know that since the two of you aren't sleeping together."

She shot him a look from under her lashes. "That's subject to change at any time."

That rocked him, even as the regret crept into her eyes, but still he kept going. "Not if I can help it. Damn it, Lindsay, come back to San Francisco with me."

*****

There on the deck as the lake woke to a new day and the birds sang, Lindsay gave herself a moment to relish in Brian's words, to let them flow to her heart and settle. And as he looked at her with expectant eyes, she knew he meant them. If only they were enough. "You have no idea how many times I've dreamed of hearing you say that." She walked inside and started fussing with the twisted sheets and blankets. The bedroom smelled of love, sweat and pleasure. And of Brian.

"Great. I'll do this. You start packing," he suggested gamely, grabbing a pillow off the bed.

She stilled his hands and met his gaze. "I can't go back with you, Brian. Nothing has changed."

With a nuanced turn, he brushed her lips. "Everything has changed for me. Except that I never stopped loving you."

Her breath, seamed with hope, hitched. "Everything?"

"Well, not everything." He let his hands drop and resumed his work on the bed. "But we'll work everything out, find a compromise."

The breath, along with the hope, ebbed. Still she put forth, "How? By forcing you to agree to a life you don't want? Then lose you again when you become resentful of it?" She wondered if Brian realized the whisper of prayer in her voice had been in his last night.

"No," he told her deliberately. "I'm open to marriage." He hesitated, then finished by dragging out the word, "Eventually."

"But not a family, children."

He straightened up and found her gaze. "I don't know. I don't want to make promises I can't keep."

He could surely see into her soul, his eyes penetrated so deep. She summoned every ounce of courage she had and said, "That's not enough for me."

His face became a dark, disgusted frown. "So instead you'll live a lie? Build a life on an empty promise?"

"An empty promise is better than a broken one," she told him in the surest voice she could muster. "And it's not empty; just a little empty-handed maybe. That will be remedied by building a life together."

"On a lie," Brian scoffed.

She took no umbrage at his harsh words, nor tried to refute them. She only watched him walk to the window and take in the lake absently. When he finally turned around his eyes were lackluster, his expression forlorn. "So it's still all or nothing?"

Throat aching, bones crumbling, she managed in a watery voice, "It has to be. Because anything less isn't enough for me."

He nodded slowly. "I see."

She went numb as he silently withdrew from her, from them. She reached out for him as he passed, but he flinched and shook her off. And then Lindsay knew it was really over. Because if he really loved her, really wanted her, the attorney in him would have countered.

CHAPTER THIRTEEN

A FEW DAYS LATER, PAUL walked into Brody Construction looking quite pleased with himself. "Jack around?"

"He's out on a job," Moira told him from behind her desk.

"Whereabouts?"

"Sparks."

Paul's giddiness faded. "Oh."

"Why? What's up?"

"I finished the renderings." He shook the oblong tube in his hand. "I wanted him to take a look."

"Oh, can I take a peek?" Moira hopped up. "Lindsay described the house, but I'm a visual learner. I don't have the family gene for drawing pictures in my head."

"Sure." Paul met her at the long counter separating the entrance from the cluster of desks. Pulling the end off the container, he slid out two rolls of paper. "This is just my initial drawing, of course," he explained. "Drawings, really."

"Here," Moira offered, watching Paul wrangle with the translucent paper as it curled up at the corners. "Let me help." She hadn't expected their fingertips to brush, igniting a spark that flew down her arm and settled in her stomach. She took half a step back. He gave her a startled look, as if he'd felt it too. She shook it off. "That paper can be so hard to work with." So saying, she set staplers down on the top corners of the paper.

Paul held her eyes for a few seconds, then shifted his unsettled gaze to the sketch. "I have a more detailed version on my computer at work," he began again in a businesslike tone. "But part of me still loves the feeling of transferring what I see in my mind to paper by hand. Old school, you know?"

"Yeah." Moira smiled. "I know."

"This is elevation A, with a cottage-style exterior." Paul presented, running a smoothing hand over the vellum. He folded back the paper, revealing another sheet underneath. "Then there's elevation B, which has more of a Tuscan feel."

Moira assessed the drawings one at a time. "They're both exquisite. But Lindsay will choose B," she predicted confidently, pointing to the Tuscan. "It's more contemporary." She shook her head in wonder. "And enormous."

"Five thousand square feet will seem big at first. But not for long," Paul said with a twinkle in his eye. "Before we know it, we'll have a brood of little Websters running around."

He was right and Moira might as well get used to it. She put on a happy face. "Where are you guys going to live until the house is built?"

"My place, I guess. We'll sell it eventually, though. I'll miss living on the golf course, but it's not very conducive to family life. With an acre." He pointed to the white space representing the land.

"We'll have plenty of room for a pool and a yard down the road."

"Sounds like you've got everything figured out."

"Finally. Thanks for the other day by the way. You were right. It was nothing."

Actually it had been something, Moira silently mused. But since Lindsay had sent Brian packing, seemingly for good this time, and was meeting with a caterer at this very moment, it apparently was no longer. She cleared her throat. "Lindsay said you decided on Thunderbird Lodge for the reception. I've always wondered what that place was like on the inside."

"Me too." He paused, then thought out loud excitedly, "You should have gone with Lindsay today. She's doing a taste test and finalizing the menu."

"I'll see it soon enough. Somebody has to hold down the fort around here."

He nodded in understanding. "So you vote for the Tuscan?"

Moira's eyes dropped back to the rendering. "Actually, I prefer the traditional cottage look myself. But for Lindsay, my money's on the Tuscan. She'll love the archways and the balconies."

"You're right. I don't know what I was thinking. I drew the house of my heart first, I guess."

Awkward silence hung over them for a moment. Then Moira hurriedly reminded him, "Don't forget about incorporating a fireplace. Inside and out." Her stomach twinged when she realized he wasn't looking at the drawing, but her. "That's very important to her."

"I won't." Paul swallowed hard and began rolling up the papers. "Any idea when Jack will be back?"

"No. And his cell is probably in the truck and he isn't. I can try my dad if you want."

"No, that's okay. If he's still in Sparks, it would take him too long to get there. I have to get back to the office."

Moira returned to the sanctuary of her desk and made small talk. "The foothills seem far out, but that's where all the development is heading. Hopefully, yours will be our first of many projects in that area."

"The lot is still rugged and the street is pretty rutted. And vacant, so you have to use your imagination." He reached into his pocket and checked the time on his phone. "I've got to meet the land developer there in about thirty minutes." He hesitated, then offered casually, "You could tag along if you have time."

Fortunately she didn't. "Not today. But I'll give the drafts to Jack. He'll take a look and give you a ballpark figure in the next couple of days."

"That's fine. It's not like I'm entertaining other bids or anything."

"I know. Paul, Dad would do it for free if he could."

Paul held up his hand. "I know. I also know that Jack would have done the same for me that day." Then his expression lightened. "Just think, you could have had free house calls for life."

"And a gourmet cook to boot," Moira replied with a smile.

"Your mom can hold her own. That Irish soda bread is to die for."

"Granted. But she cooked for the masses. Nothing fancy."

"Because she had the masses to cook for. I always envied you guys that way."

Moira snorted a laugh. "At least you could hear yourself think at your house."

"Yeah, we always want what we don't have." Paul slid the rolls of paper into the cylinder. "Don't we?"

Indeed, Moira thought with an internal kick, realizing she was wringing her hands in her lap. "It looks like you're going to make up for it."

"Got lucky there. Lindsay wants a big family too. To make up for being an only child."

"Be careful what you wish for," Moira advised. "I babysat my nephews last night." She wiped her brow with the back of her hand theatrically and reclined in the leather swivel. "I'm exhausted today."

"You do look a little tired. I figured you had a hot date or something."

If Moira didn't know better, she'd swear he was fishing. "Hardly."

He flashed that million dollar smile, the one that made Moira's stomach do somersaults. She'd seen it all her life, but never really took note of it until recently. Paul's teeth looked as white as winter's first snow against his olive skin and his dark eyes gleamed in perfect complement. She watched him tap the cylinder against the counter and replace the cap.

He found her stare and holding it briefly asked, "Should I leave these here or throw them on Jack's desk?"

She shook off the reverie. "There is fine. He won't forget about them if they're sitting out," Moira answered, taking refuge in her computer monitor.

"Then I guess I'm out of here. I'll touch base in a couple days."

"Sounds good." And as much as she hated to admit it, Moira knew she would look forward to that.

CHAPTER FOURTEEN

AUTUMN'S YOUTH HAD INUNDATED the Sierras with vibrant reds and oranges while fields of wildflowers flooded the hills with color. Nestled under a blinding blue sky, Mother Nature presented herself as the perfect backdrop for an outdoor wedding.

"Thank you for altering the dress for me," Lindsay told the white-haired woman with whom she shared the trifold mirror.

"It's an honor," Mary Agnes Donahue replied, slipping a delicate hand behind the row of satin covered buttons on the corset. "What are the chances of working on the same gown twice? You didn't find the veil?"

"I went through all the boxes in the attic twice. There wasn't anything else but wedding photos."

"The silk tulle doesn't age well without being preserved anyway. The one you chose is just as lovely. And you've got plenty of sentiment with the dress. Besides, the whole is always worth more than its pieces."

Taking that in with a nod, Lindsay watched the other woman round the podium, pin cushion at her hip, and arrange the chapel train.

"It should lay better now after being out of the box for two months." Stepping back, she pressed the palms of her hands together and triumphed, "Stunning, if I do say so myself."

Swallowing the lump in her throat, Lindsay gazed at her reflection. The sweetheart neckline gave way to a bodice of hammered pearls and a satin skirt trimmed in silk ribbon. "It's absolutely beautiful. I don't know what to say."

"You're beautiful. Just like your mother."

So Lindsay had always heard. "I wish I could remember more."

"About your parents? Grace told you about them, showed you pictures, right?"

"She did. But sometimes it's hard to distinguish between my memories and hers."

Mrs. Donahue pulled at the excess material on the back of the corset. "Then don't. They're all good."

Was it selfish to want her own memories? "I do remember some things. Like roasting s'mores at the lake with my mother in the summer. And my father's hands."

"His hands?"

"I remember him washing my little hands in his big ones, making a game out of it with the bubbles. I used to dream about that, about them all the time. I'd wake up and expect them to be there. But they never were."

"Things happen for a reason." She spoke through a commiserating smile. "Somehow we have to believe that."

"But what reason could there have been to take them both?" Lindsay contemplated the carnation pink carpeting and finished quietly, "And leave me all alone."

"You weren't alone. You had your grandmother. It was probably for the best that..." She swallowed the words.

Lindsay's head snapped up. "For the best that what?"

"Your parents loved each other very much," Mrs. Donahue explained. "It's for the best that they died together."

Lindsay was appalled. "More than they loved me?"

"No, no, of course not," she qualified briskly, fussing with the charmeuse. "You are that love." She paused as if mentally rewinding time. "When your mom worked in my shop, your dad ran deliveries for the merchants on the mountain. All of my material was shipped into Reno then, so he came by two or three times a week. I had the privilege of watching their love bloom." Her pale blue eyes looked around the room absently. "Sometimes our soul mates are who we least expect. True love is funny that way. Some people never find it." Her atrophied hands rested. "I never did."

The old woman's tone was so earnest, so heartfelt, that Lindsay had to take a moment. "But you married, had a family."

"Oh, yes. And I loved my husband dearly. Those were different times; that's what you did then." She pushed away the melancholy and resumed her work. "We had a wonderful life, four children and a slew of grandchildren. But there was always something missing. Your parents had that missing piece," she said, completing her loop around Lindsay. "And now so do you."

Lindsay sent her a counterfeit smile, feeling another piece of her heart break off. But she would pick it up and put it back together as she had the others and move forward. She'd been correct in assuming she wouldn't hear from Brian again. Her indiscretion still haunted her and hardly a night went by without him entering her dreams. Her comeuppance, she supposed. But Paul was there too, as if waiting in the wings. Sometimes amid the backdrop of their new house. Or the lake on a glorious summer day. Brian, on the contrary, walked in the shadows. Hand outstretched, he would come toward her. But just before he reached her, she would jar awake breathless, heart racing and dripping in sweat.

"Have you lost weight?" Mrs. Donahue was asking, tugging at the bodice. "Or have my pins shifted?"

Lindsay returned to the conversation. "Maybe. I started working with the Brodys.

Between that and the wedding, I've been too busy to eat much. Plus I had a nasty stomach bug."

"Has to be a good six or seven pounds," she speculated through the pins between her teeth. "Try not to lose anymore. Has your system righted itself?"

"It's the oddest thing. Some days I'm starving, others the mere thought of food turns my stomach."

A brief silence fell over the fitting room and Mrs. Donahue shook her head imperceptibly, then changed the subject. "What are you doing for the Brodys?"

"Interior design consultation. Free of charge, to build a clientele."

"Weren't you getting your MBA?"

"Yeah. I switched gears."

"That's probably more conducive to family life anyway. How's the house coming?"

"Great. They're hoping to have the foundation poured before the weather turns," Lindsay answered, following the silent direction to step down.

"You should have some time on that. Moira's dress came in yesterday." Her voice was circumspect. "Would you let her know?"

"Sure." Lindsay stepped out of the gown. "She wanted to come in today. To see me in the dress. She must have gotten tied up at work."

"The timing is tight, so I'll need to see her this week." The seamstress started to say something else, but abandoned it. Instead, she smiled warily, her eyes full of intuition and misgiving, and spread the heirloom on the sewing table.

Lindsay dressed and joined her. Then, with a sudden sinking feeling in her stomach, asked, "Mrs. Donahue, is there something wrong? Or something you're not telling me?"

"Just now? Oh no, dear. Just a senior moment."

"You don't have senior moments."

Drawing an indecisive breath, she admitted, "I was just thinking that I'm losing my touch." She ran her hands over the tiny pearls. "Now, where was that cracked one?"

"Hardly." Lindsay gestured around the dressing area filled with racks of dresses and body forms.

"I mean when it comes to reading people," she explained, marking the imperfection with blue chalk. "I had Moira pegged all wrong. If one of you were to marry the Webster boy, my money would have been on her."

Lindsay's jaw dropped to the floor as the other woman shook her head and continued. "I should have known better. She always had a thing for him, but he only had eyes for you."

CHAPTER FIFTEEN

MRS. DONAHUE WAS WRONG. About the weather anyway, Lindsay mused, wrapping the cardigan tighter around herself and crossing her arms over her chest as she walked through the cemetery. Moira, however, was an entirely different matter. Arriving on the heels of Mrs. Donahue's stunning observation, her friend cheerfully announced her plan to take the rest of the day off to enjoy a final summer afternoon on the beach. Then, proudly modeling the black chiffon attendant's dress, she repeatedly apologized for not making it in time for Lindsay's fitting. It wasn't that Moira was acting at all oddly; she was disturbingly normal. It was the martyred look in her eyes. Had it been there all along? And the cadence of her words. Was her voice always that high-pitched?

They'd spent the remainder of the day soaking up September's fleeting rays of sunshine before sharing a bottle of wine and going over some preliminary interior sketches of the house. Moira was chattier than usual; so much so that Lindsay couldn't get a word in edgewise. Which was fine because she had nothing to say. Nothing to say to her best friend in the world, the only constant in her life, with whom she had a lifetime in common. Perhaps more than she knew.

The caretaker, a short, stout man with deep-set eyes and a grizzly disposition, greeted Lindsay by name. Refusing his passive offer of coffee from his thermos, she continued down the well-traveled footpath. It was so peaceful here in the back, among the silhouettes of the aspens and white firs, an occasional pine. Lindsay was the lone visitor in the cemetery this morning.

"I've been here a lot lately, huh Gram?" she said, plopping down on the sandstone bench. "You told me not to bother; I could talk to you from anywhere. But I always feel closer to you here." She rubbed her hands together, then blew on them. "I thought I was over that nasty flu, but today it seems to be back. Payback for the Cab Moira and I drank last night, I guess." She tucked her legs beneath her with a dismissive snicker. "I know, I know, this too shall pass. But there's something that won't go away. That little voice inside my head. The one you told me never to ignore. I willed it quiet for a while, busying myself with the remodeling, then the wedding and my new business. But now it's back, louder than ever. And yesterday I realized it wasn't my voice at all. It was yours. Your voice in my dreams about Brian, your voice challenging my illusions of a life with Paul. Bet you had something to do with my conversation with Mrs. Donahue yesterday, too."

"Well, you finally got my attention, Gram. Not with your voice, but with your eyes. I saw Moira through your eyes yesterday for the first time. And I was humbled. Incredibly humbled that you had to go that far for me to listen." Rising, she plucked a weed from the base of the shiny black marble of the gravestone and shucked it to the side. She would need to replace the impatiens with pansies sooner rather than later if this weather proved telling. Brushing the dirt off her palms, she plowed on. "I never would have thought it, Moira and Paul. But, I decided at three o'clock this morning, it makes perfect sense. The scary part is the idea didn't even bother me. It sat just fine. What upset me was that I was too blind to see it before. Any of it." She spun the homemade bangle on her wrist. "Like when I came to tell you about Paul proposing, my ambivalence about it. Then I found Mom's dress in the attic and took that as a sign from you. But that was just insurance. You knew I'd go to Mrs. Donahue," she alleged, beginning to pace. Then you arranged for Brian's reappearance in my life. I sent him away, not once, but twice. But that last time." Lindsay felt the tears building as melancholy engulfed her throat. "I just couldn't. Because I love him so much. And I know he loves me too. It was woven into his eyes, his words, his touch, that night."

"So why isn't that enough? Why do I have to choose between the man I love and the life I want? Until yesterday I'd convinced myself that I didn't. Because a man I love in a different way can give me both. I could have gone on pretending to believe that. Gone on lying to myself. Until now. Because it's just not about me anymore." Sniffling, she patted the butter-colored wool in search of a tissue. Instead something sharp pricked her. "Ah," she huffed, biting back the sting. "What's with the damn sea glass? Another random piece," she said, throwing it aside, "you can't do anything with." Lindsay swiped a hand across her cheeks in lieu of a tissue, amazed that the worthless trinket didn't shatter on the sidewalk. She stared at it as beams of daybreak burst through the trees, filling the air with coronas and sunspots. Hunching down, she flipped the beveled glass over in her palm. It was shaped unlike any other piece she'd seen; oblong and pointy, yet thick and sturdy. Whisking away the tiny strands of lint from the edges, she studied it for a few moments more, then tossed it in her purse.

"You're playing dirty now, Gram, involving Moira." Resuming her rant, Lindsay straightened up. "No wonder she was so aloof when I told her Brian had invited me to San Francisco. She was no doubt tortured, knowing telling me what I needed to hear would be self-serving. So she tried to make me see it for myself. But I was oblivious," she scolded herself, looking out over the rows of tombstones lined up like soldiers in the dawn light. "She knew what I refused to admit. That I'm afraid. Afraid to be alone, afraid to admit that I already am. Afraid to let Brian love me the way I love him in case someday he's not enough. Afraid to let myself love Brian in case I lose him too. Like my parents and you. And now maybe Moira. So I heard what I wanted to hear and went on kidding myself. But you wouldn't stand for that. Now you've forced me to see how foolish I've been. I kept asking you for a sign, something to guide me, push me to do the right thing. And it was hidden in plain sight all along." She looked down and kicked the thin, sparse grass in front of the grave. "Hell, for all I know, Paul feels something for Moira and is just as oblivious to it as I was to her feelings for him. Maybe they're destined to be together and I'm screwing that up too."

Lindsay dropped back down on the bench defeatedly. "But the arrangements are made, cake ordered, invitations sent. We bought the most incredible lot, are going to build on it. And I finally got my ring." She flashed her hand in the air in front of her. "It's stunning, isn't it? Just like the dress. But you already knew that." She let out a measured breath and bargained on with hushed reverence. "What will I tell him, Gram? It's not you, it's me. And by the way, Moira is in love with you. He'll think I've lost my damn mind. And she would be mortified. If she hasn't told me, she surely hasn't told anyone else." She listened to the birds greet the day for a long moment. Then she stood and decided under her breath, "So I guess I'll just tell him the truth. Most of it anyway." Lindsay bid her grandmother goodbye and retraced her steps, making a plan as she went.

*****

The restaurant was bustling, filled with the rushed lunch hour crowd. "Can I start you off with a drink, ma'am? Two for one well drinks, beer and house wine."

"Just iced tea for me," Lindsay told the middle-aged woman who had appeared over her shoulder.

She smiled in acknowledgement and walked away just as Paul arrived, phone to his ear. The perfect package, Lindsay reminded herself as he approached her. Except for that one missing piece.

"Hi," he mouthed, kissing her cheek. "Yeah, let me know what happens." He ended the conversation and took a seat across from Lindsay. "Sorry."

"No problem. You said it would be a week from hell."

"As advertised. How about you?" he asked as the waitress returned.

Paul's drink order and the distribution of menus gave Lindsay a moment to brace herself. She waited for the other woman to leave, then began with a deep breath. "I've had quite a week myself. I went to the cemetery today."

"I'll never understand why they built a cemetery on that land," Paul interjected, opening his menu.

"It's prime real estate. I guess during the Gold Rush they weren't thinking about lake views and building codes. I'm surprised a developer hasn't bought it and relocated the graves." He shot her an apologetic grin. "But I digress. What were you saying?"

"I guess you're right. I've never thought of it as anything other than a cemetery," she replied absently. "Anyway, I've been doing some thinking." She hesitated, tucked a few strands of hair behind her ear and cleared her throat. "About the wedding."

He gave her an inquisitive look over the top of the menu. "Oh? How so?"

She straightened her shoulders, lifted her chin and spat out, "I don't think there should be one."

Shock flashed into his eyes before they narrowed. Mouth agape, he lowered the menu slowly. "What? Why?"

Just then the waitress returned. "Ready to order, folks?"

"I think we need a minute." Paul's reply was unduly curt.

"Of course." She deposited the drinks and moved on to the next table.

Lindsay had never felt so low, watching him look at her in complete disbelief. "Because it would be dishonest, selfish and unfair."

"Because..."

"Because." She swallowed hard. "I still have feelings for Brian."

"What kind of feelings?" Paul demanded, dropping the menu on the table.

Lindsay sucked in a breath and said, "I'm still in love with him."

"I see," he shot back angrily after what seemed like an eternity. "And how long has all of this been going on?"

"Nothing's going on," she lied, crossing her fingers under the table. "I've tried to forget him, get over him. But I can't. At least not yet."

Paul's dark eyes went cold and shark-like. "And do you expect me to wait around until you do?"

Shaking inside, Lindsay managed to hold his steely gaze. "No."

"So that's it?" he snapped. "After years of friendship and so much more. You meet me for lunch to say you have unresolved feelings for an old boyfriend. One whom, until two months ago, you supposedly hadn't had contact with in over a year." Leaning back in his chair, he folded his arms across his chest. "One who broke your heart. Shamelessly. Are you trying to right that wrong? Is he?"

"No. Brian doesn't know anything about this."

She watched shock roll across his face. Then he gave her a curious look and asked, "Why now, then?"

"I kept thinking my feelings would go away," she said, trying to convince herself as much as him. "Resolve themselves. That it was seeing him again. But now I know it's not that simple. We're approaching the point of no return. I'd be marrying you under false pretenses. I love you too much to do that."

"Apparently not," Paul piqued, standing.

The hurt was planted firmly in his eyes now and spreading like wildfire. Lindsay jumped up and grabbed his arm. "But I do! I know I do! I'm just not *in* love with you."

Shaking free, he reached into his pocket and retrieved his wallet. "That's too bad. Because I would have loved you forever." He threw a few bills on the table and started to walk away, then paused. "You're not marrying me, not going to him. Have you thought about where that leaves you, Lindsay?" He turned on his heel and marched out of the restaurant.

She watched his retreating back in mortified wonder for a few heart-pounding beats before slumping back into the chair and burying her face in her hands.

"Can I get you anything else?"

Lindsay turned her head toward the tentative voice. "Ah, no. I'm sorry we tied up the table." And inadvertently made a scene in the process. She reached for her bag and retrieved her wallet. "Here, this should cover everything."

"It looks like the gentleman already took care of it," the waitress pointed out gently, picking up the bills on the table.

"Oh, yes, of course." Lindsay started to stand up, but the room began to spin, forcing her to reconsider.

"Easy there, honey. You okay?"

"Yeah, just a little dizzy."

"Here," she directed, "drink some tea."

"No," Lindsay declined, waving the glass away. "I'll be fine in a minute. This has been happening a bit lately. It always passes."

"All right." The waitress looked at her skeptically. Then as if to justify her continued presence, commented, "Your ring is beautiful."

"Thank you," Lindsay accepted, too spent to dispute the compliment.

"Mine wasn't much more than a chip," she related with a nostalgic smile. "But I loved it. Picked it out myself."

"Loved?" Lindsay inquired tiredly, noticing only a plain gold band on the other woman's left hand.

"It slipped off at the beach one day. Washed away with the current. I was sick about it for the longest time." She shrugged carelessly. "Then I realized he was what mattered, not a silly piece of glass."

"Yeah," Lindsay agreed. "I guess you're right."

The woman shifted her attention in the direction of a beckoning voice. "Stay as long as you like. Let me know if I can bring you anything else."

After a few minutes of staring into space, Lindsay reached into her purse and dug for her keys. Instead she found the sea glass trinket she'd come upon at the cemetery earlier. "You're not going to get me anywhere," she sighed in frustration. But for some reason, she threw it in her change purse for safekeeping.

*****

"You must be freezing out there," came a disembodied voice from behind.

Keeping her gaze on the boats bouncing off the dark water, Lindsay conceded, "It is getting a little chilly."

"Before you know it, the dock will be empty. Nice long summer this year, though.

Problem is, we're skipping fall and going right into winter."

She tossed an easy smile over her shoulder at the man she'd known for as long as she could remember and threw a pebble into the lake. It rippled, creating soft undulations on the surface. She watched as the waves dissipated and the water flattened again.

"That's gotta be a dozen or so by now. Come on in. Get something to warm you up."

He was right; about the stones and the cold. She rubbed the sides of her arms and turned around. Mac was standing on the hotel's back deck, holding the door open. "Thanks," she told him, walking through the threshold.

"I should be thanking you. Wednesday evenings are usually reserved for dry businessmen from Eureka," he said, gray eyes sparkling from behind the whiskers of time. "What's your pleasure? Coffee? Hot chocolate? Wine?"

"Hot chocolate would be great." She settled herself on one of the bar stools and swept the restaurant with her eyes. "Slow tonight, huh?"

"Typical weeknight in the shoulder season," Mac answered from behind the bar. "How have you been?"

"Okay. You?"

"Busy. I've been working six or seven nights a week all summer," he replied, entering the order in the computer. Then turning to face her, added, "Matter of fact, I met a friend of yours not long ago."

"Who? You know everybody I know around here."

"He wasn't from around here. He was from San Francisco."

"Oh," she sobered, looking down at her hands. "Brian."

"Had to be a good two months ago now."

"Fourth of July."

"That was it," Mac affirmed with a nod. "The two of us had quite a chat."

Lindsay felt herself stiffen. "What did you and Brian have to chat about?"

"This and that. I told him my story, he told me his. Helluva nice guy. A little lost though."

That had Lindsay's head popping up in wonder. "Brian? Lost?"

"Just my opinion, not a criticism," Mac hastily qualified. "I guess he's not lost so much as he is looking for something." His tone was allusive. "Or someone."

Lindsay watched the man old enough to be her father step aside, allowing the waitress to set a mug topped with a mound of whipped cream down on the bar in front of her. She smiled in acknowledgement, then returned to Mac. "No, Brian doesn't need anyone. He likes his life just the way it is."

"Or so he's tried to convince himself. And apparently you've done the same."

"I'm not convinced of anything anymore," Lindsay admitted, twisting the broken promise on her finger.

She felt Mac's eyes study her for a moment before he began speaking again. "You know, your grandparents came in a lot when I first started working here."

"So I've heard," she replied, wondering what that had to do with anything, but grateful Mac had changed the subject.

"Some people have all the luck."

"Gram always did have card sense." Smiling at the memory, Lindsay lifted her gaze and took a cautious sip of the hot chocolate. "Unfortunately, that proclivity was lost on me. I can't win for losing."

"I don't mean at the tables," Mac clarified. "I mean with each other. Even a bitter, down on his luck alcoholic could see how your grandparents felt about one another." Leaning in, he rested his forearms on the bar. "You and Brian looked at each other the same way on the stairs that night. Like you were the only ones in the room. That's how I knew he was the one."

"What one?" Lindsay asked as the milk warmed her insides.

"The guy from San Francisco who broke your heart."

Stunned, Lindsay could only gawk at him.

"Don't forget what a small town this is when the tourists go home." He straightened up with a knowing grin.

After a few silent clicks, Lindsay grunted, "We broke each other's hearts."

"That's what he said."

Her eyes began to sting. "He did?"

"Yeah." His gaze went to her left hand, frozen in midair. "And he hoped it wasn't too late to put them back together."

"Brian said that?" Hope and apprehension were at it again, spinning around in her stomach like a disparate top.

Mac's kind eyes were pinned on hers again. "Not in so many words. But the message passed between us. It'd be a shame if it stopped there."

Awestruck, she watched him walk away and greet the patrons arriving at the far end of the bar. She considered the mug in her hand, but her churning stomach had her pushing it away without a second sip. Retrieving her purse from the back of the stool, she pulled out her wallet. And with it the sea glass she'd discovered this morning. "You're like a bad penny, aren't you?" she muttered to herself, tracing its jagged edges with her finger. Then, as if the forgotten trinket was beckoning to her through the rays of light bouncing off it, Lindsay shifted her eyes to the makeshift bracelet on her wrist. Sliding it off, she untwisted the wire, attached the straggler piece and retied. *The whole is always worth more than its pieces.* Mrs. Donahue's words rang in her ears. Suddenly seeing things clearly for the first time, she bid Mac goodbye and ran out into the cold night, with her wish still on her lips.

CHAPTER SIXTEEN

LINDSAY HAD TO TALK herself out of leaving that very minute. But Gram was at it again, reminding her how treacherous the mountain roads could be at night. It seemed hard to believe that snow flurries were flying when a day ago she and Moira had been baking in the sun. Inescapable exhaustion finally took over, and when she woke the morning was clear and crisp. The dusting of snow had framed the mountains and alpine meadows, reminding Lindsay of the powdered sugar sprinkled French toast her grandmother used to make. Only an occasional house dotted the wall of trees that lined the road on this part of the mountain, something with which she could identify. It had crossed her mind more than once that her life-altering epiphany might not be welcomed. Or too late, she thought as the phone rang for the third time.

"Brody and Sons Construction."

"I wanted to let you know I'm on my way to San Francisco," she informed Moira by way of greeting.

"Well, hello to you too."

"Sorry." She began again, "Hello."

"That's better. So what takes you to San Francisco so suddenly? Transcripts?"

School was the last thing on Lindsay's mind. "Hardly." She paused, then spit out, "I broke off the engagement." For the first time in her life, Lindsay had no idea what her friend was thinking. Was she secretly, guiltily relieved? Shocked? Confused?

Moira's breath hitched. "You what?"

"You heard me. I'm taking your advice."

"*My* advice?"

"To follow my heart. As corny as it sounds, I left it in San Francisco. And I'm going to try to get it back."

There was dead air on the other end of the line. Then Moira ground out, "And what brought on this sudden change of heart?"

That, Lindsay decided, was for another day. "It's not as sudden as it seems. I've been doing a lot of thinking lately. I've been going through the motions, kidding myself. Forcing myself to feel what I want to feel. Not what I really do feel." Her voice sounded surprisingly reasonable.

"That's a lot of thinking for a day or two. Or even a month or two. Maybe it's just cold feet."

"I tried that one. I also tried the devil's advocate bullshit you used on me in the yard that day. But it all comes down to one thing."

Moira laughed a little, seemingly in spite of herself. "Which is?"

"I can't marry Paul when I'm still in love with Brian," she acknowledged out loud, toying with the string of diamonds on her wrist.

After another grueling lull, Moira said, "I guess that's hard for me to fathom. I've never been in love, let alone with two men at once."

But you have! You are! Lindsay screamed inside. "That's it, Moirs. I'm not. I love Paul, but I'm not *in* love with him. Something is missing."

There was another brief silence during which Lindsay pictured Moira threading a pen through her fingers and staring unseeingly at her computer screen. Finally she put in, "How did Paul take it?"

"Predictably. It was one of the hardest things I've ever done."

"Why didn't you call me?"

"I had to handle this solo. Something I might have to get used to."

"I doubt that. How long will you be in San Francisco?"

"A few hours to the rest of my life. I'll let you know when I know." Lindsay cut the wheel to the right and slowed down, but still took the curve too fast, allowing the diamond bracelet to reunite with its sea glass companion.

"You haven't told Brian?" Moira astonished.

"No," Lindsay answered, pushing down the panic. "And for all I know, it's too late."

*****

"Brian!" Brian stopped walking and pivoted in the direction of the husky voice. The mocha wrap thrown over Reese Ramsey's shoulders matched her eyes, rich in innuendo. Her honey blonde hair was swept into a flawless twist and the multitude of bracelets adorning her wrists clanged merrily as she sidled up to him. "How wonderful to see you," she purred. "I trust you got my messages. You must speak with your assistant; she's a bit territorial. I explained who I was more than once."

"Reese," Brian greeted, pecking each of her silky cheeks. "You look fabulous as usual." He made a mental note to tease Jan about her message filtration. "What brings you to San Francisco?"

"Oh, just some papers to sign. A formality really." She waved a dismissive hand in the air, the devil dancing in her eyes. "How did you know I was staying here?" she asked, tracing his lips with a perfectly manicured nail.

Same old Reese, assuming the world revolved around her. "I didn't," he told her with a chuckle. "I'm here to meet a client. All of our out-of-town business stays here."

"In that case, let me buy you a drink until your client…" She raised her eyebrows as if speaking in code, "arrives. Or better yet, maybe I'll get lucky and you'll get stood up," she propositioned, pressing herself against him and wreathing his neck with her arms.

"Sorry, Reese," Brian declined, grabbing her wrists. "Not this time."

"Well, then, perhaps your friend could join us," she conspired roguishly. "Any friend of yours is a friend of mine." Her tongue moved across her ruby red lips in a long, lazy stroke.

Brian clenched his jaw and remained strangely impervious. "I don't think so."

"Oh, come now. We used to have so much fun together." She brought his hands down to her waist and held them there. "I'll be in town for a while, indefinitely really. How about tomorrow?"

"I'm going to L.A. tomorrow."

"When you get back then." Leaning forward, she pinned her mouth to his. She tasted as sultry as she looked.

Brian had no desire to take her up on her offer of casual, meaningless sex. Even as she pushed at him, thoughts of Lindsay's body pinned against his flooded his mind, his heart, his cock, no doubt giving Reese the wrong impression. He assumed his hands and took two steps backward. "You have no idea how hard it is for me to say this, but I'm going to pass."

"I do, actually." She lowered her eyes to his midsection and gave him a chagrined look before reaching into her clutch and pulling out a business card. "Here are my numbers. If you change your mind give me a call. Anytime. Day or night."

"These must be hot off the presses," he commented, noting the name at the top of the card. "Was it husband number two or three?"

"Three, darling. And the third time was definitely *not* the charm." With humor shinning in her eyes, she turned on her stilettos and swaggered toward the elevators.

"It was nice to see you," Brian called to her retreating back.

She stopped and cocked her head to the side. "You too." She stared at him appraisingly for a few seconds, then went on. "Tell me something. Am I losing my touch or is your client friend that special?"

Brian felt his expression collapse. "You're not losing your touch, Reese. Not at all."

*****

"Checking in ma'am?" asked a man in an impeccably pressed crimson uniform trimmed in gold. The whirl of a dozen flags cutting the wind snapped above, not to be outdone by the clanking of cable cars.

"I am," Lindsay informed him, sounding more sure than she felt inside.

"Welcome to the Fairmont," the salt and pepper-haired valet said, handing her a numbered ticket. "Will you need your car later this evening?"

She gave the bracelets dangling from her wrist an uncertain glance. "I'm not sure."

"Park it around the corner for now," he directed a younger man dressed in similar attire, then addressed Lindsay again, "Just let the concierge know if you do. Otherwise we'll move it to the overnight lot in a few hours. I'll be right behind you with your bag."

"Thank you," she said as the revolving door swept her into the gilded lobby outfitted with palace columns and marble floors. She lifted her gaze from the opulent wrought iron staircase when she realized the valet was talking to her.

"First time in San Francisco?"

"No, I used to live here," she answered, noting the brass nameplate on his lapel.

An odd sense of understanding flashed into the man's gentle eyes. "San Francisco can be a hard place to live. But it's an even harder place to leave. I guess Tony Bennett said it best."

"Yeah," Lindsay agreed under her breath. "I guess he did."

Charlie gave her a warm smile, then extended one arm out in front of him in silent invitation to continue toward the reception desk.

Her heels echoed on the polished floor, blending with the hum of voices and the chime of elevators coming and going. She'd thought about going to Brian's apartment, being there when he got home. But this was safer. She was pinning her hopes on an offer made in the heat of passion, months ago. And if that offer no longer stood, Brian would never have to know she'd been here at all.

"Good evening," the enthusiastic clerk greeted. "Do you have a reservation?"

Bracing herself to be embarrassed, she answered with feigned confidence, "I believe so. Lindsay Foster. It might be under Cummings and—"

"Yes, I have you right here, Ms. Foster," the young man broke in. "Considering today's availability, I can offer you a room in the Tower building. Would you prefer a bay or city view?"

He looked at her expectantly, having no idea how his words wooed her. She let out a sharp breath. "Either," she replied, feeling the corners of her mouth break into a smile. "What do you suggest?"

"I prefer the bay myself, but I'm here on Nob Hill everyday."

"Then the bay it is."

"Fill this out, please," he directed before addressing the bellman. "Ms. Foster will be staying in one of our Signature rooms."

Obliging, Lindsay picked up the pen that lay in front of her on the counter. She'd barely written her name when a throaty laugh filled the lobby, drawing her attention. Instantly, the crescent shape of her lips turned downward and she froze in place as the pen fell to the floor.

Brian wore black pants and a blue dress shirt. Poured into a siren-red dress, the woman stared solicitously into his eyes and leaned against him on the most beautiful legs Lindsay had ever seen. She watched Brian slide his hands down the woman's curvy torso and rest them on her waist. And then, in what seemed like slow motion, slant down to kiss her. That sent ice water rushing through her veins and a pike into her chest that surely pierced her lung.

"Ms. Foster? Is there a problem?"

Heart lodged in her throat, Lindsay shifted her gaze to the man behind the desk. "Ah, no. But I'm not going to need the room after all," she told him, tearing the registration card in half.

"If you aren't satisfied with the Tower I can—"

"It has nothing to do with the accommodations," Lindsay interrupted. "My plans have suddenly changed. I'll need my car, please." She had to will her voice steady.

The bellman and clerk exchanged a curious look. Then the former picked up her bag and said, "Yes, of course. I'll have it brought right up."

"Thank you." Looking out the corner of her eye as she bent to retrieve the pen, she gave silent thanks for no further sign of Brian and his companion. She stood, placed the pen on the counter and gave the clerk a perfunctory smile. "I'm sorry. Thank you again." Then, shaking as jaggedly as the paper she'd torn, she retraced her steps as fast as her legs would carry her.

"Change your mind, ma'am?" Charlie asked as she stepped out under the red canopy.

"Yeah," she replied, as the tears stung her eyes. "But it was too late."

She let the tears fall as she hurriedly put the car in gear to drive away, oblivious to Charlie's parting warning about the fog rolling in particularly thick on the bridges tonight.

CHAPTER SEVENTEEN

"THANK YOU," BRIAN TOLD his ex-wife the next day as they walked along the shady path in front of Kelsey's dorm.

"For what?"

"For raising such a wonderful person. For giving me the greatest part of my life. When was the last time I thanked you?"

Laura stopped and gave him a suspicious look. "Right back at you. What's gotten into you?"

"Can't a man tell the mother of his only child how much he appreciates her?"

"Of course. But not this man." She regarded him for a long moment and then, hazel eyes wide, exclaimed, "Oh, no! Are you sick?"

"No, I'm fine," Brian told her around a chuckle. "Thanks for the concern anyway."

"What then?"

Brian took a moment to study Laura. She still looked like the girl he had fallen in love with all those years ago. Her sable hair fell against a heart-shaped face bearing only the faintest sign of lifelines and her golden skin was still as taut as the frame it encased. In all his soul-searching lately, he realized he'd known Laura longer than anyone in his life. And that she probably knew him better than anyone ever had. "Did you love me?" he asked, hoping he already knew the answer.

"Yes, of course," she responded easily. "I will always love you."

"Really?"

"Yes, really. You are my first love, my daughter's father." Her tone grew soulful.

"Obviously you don't feel the same way or you wouldn't have to ask."

"I do feel that way," he told her and meant it. "So what happened between us?"

"We weren't in love with each other anymore. There are all kinds of love. Ours wasn't the kind to last a lifetime."

"And you and Tom have the lifetime kind?"

Shrugging, she answered mildly, "Yeah."

"How did you know the difference?"

Her eyes searched the near distance. Then she returned to him saying, "It wasn't love at first sight, like with you. It evolved over time." She took a moment to find the words. "Like finally solving a riddle or finding the missing piece to a puzzle."

That was a little deep for Brian, but he got the point. "How is your relationship with Tom different from ours?"

"Well, we aren't twenty and poor and living in student housing," she shot back with a laugh. Then her face sobered and her eyes misted. "But God, was I happy," she said and touched his cheek. He rested his hand on hers, the words soothing him like a vintage ballad.

Putting her arm through Brian's, she started walking again. "I guess the biggest difference is that you and I didn't share a life. We lived two parallel lives together. I blamed myself for that for a long time after we separated."

"Why?"

"I shared my life with you, but you didn't share yours with me. It wasn't your fault; you didn't know how. I should have showed you. I had an example of that with my parents. You didn't." As if pocketing the blame, she elaborated, "Law school, working, having a baby earlier than we expected. It was a trial by fire." She gave him a hopeful look. "Have you met someone?"

How do women know these things? "Remember Lindsay?"

"Oh, yes. Kelsey thought you might actually settle down. Have you reconciled?"

Brian stopped walking and sat on a bench under a huge oak tree. He rested his elbows on his thighs, his chin on his knuckles. "Not really. She's younger; wants to get married, have a family."

Laura joined him. "And you don't."

For some reason he didn't say no, just shrugged his shoulders and kept his eyes on his shoes.

"I was that bad, huh?" she asked sheepishly.

"Stop." He shot that down and turned to face her. "I'm just too old, too busy for all of that."

Laura held his eyes for a few moments before her lips curved victoriously. "Brian Rembrandt, you're afraid."

"I am not!" he charged back, straightening up.

"Yes, you are. Your pragmatic mind can't control your fanciful heart. So you're playing the marriage/kids/lifestyle card to protect yourself." She sat back, crossed her arms and the haughty smile broadened. "Wow, you must really love this girl."

"I guess I do." The words escaped his lips without warning.

"And she loves you too but is just as stubborn?"

"So stubborn she's marrying someone else."

She shook her head and raised her eyes to the sky. "What a pair you two make. Your children are going to be quite a challenge to raise."

"Didn't you hear me? Lindsay is getting married," he reminded her sarcastically. "To another man."

Laura seemed to find that irrelevant. "Only if you let her."

Unable to sit still any longer, Brian jumped up. "I tried! I went to her, tried to get her back. She refused." Looking at his feet, he kicked the grass defeatedly. "Apparently I'm not enough for her."

"So that's it?" Laura said, rising along with her voice. "The youngest attorney ever to become a partner at one of San Francisco's oldest and most respected law firms just throws in the towel." She put a dramatic hand out in the air in front of her.

"What if you'd done that with me? We wouldn't be sitting here today."

"That was different. We were kids and that guy you were seeing was a jerk." Brian waved away the analogy. "Con Law was a bitch; he wanted free tutoring." He ran his fingers through his hair and began to pace. "Conversely, Lindsay's fiancé has it all. He," Brian made air quotes and finished mockingly, "can give her everything she's ever wanted."

She gave him a deliberate stare, indulging his self-pity session for a few seconds before taking him by the shoulders. "No, he can't. Not if she loves you half as much as you love her. And she must or you wouldn't. Don't let her go, Brian," she implored. "You'll regret it for the rest of your life. What are you really afraid of?"

Clasping her forearms, he searched the eyes that mirrored his daughter's. "What if we fall out of love too?"

Laura looked back at him, her eyes shining with possibility, and whispered, "But what if you don't?"

CHAPTER EIGHTEEN

THE PHONE WAS ALREADY ringing when Moira walked into the office the next morning. Leaving the keys in the door, she disarmed the alarm and dove across the desk. "Fine," she said to no one as the dial tone buzzed in her ear. She threw down her purse, unwittingly dumping half of its contents on the chair. Blowing her bangs out of her eyes and swearing under her breath, she decided coffee was the first order of business. She flipped on the TV and began scooping the grounds into the coffee maker. The metrologist threw to the anchor for a final check of the local news before segueing to the *Today Show*. "To recap our top story, all eastbound lanes of the San Francisco-Oakland Bay Bridge remain closed. The bridge was shut down last evening due to a thirty-car pileup. Among the dozens injured are three known fatalities."

"What a mess," Moira thought out loud as the phone started ringing again. Luckily Lindsay would have made it to San Francisco before the accident. And would have been traveling in the opposite direction. "Brody and Sons Construction." Landline tucked into her shoulder, she tossed her sunglasses back into the oversized bag.

"Yes, hello," said a female voice. "This is San Francisco Memorial Hospital. We're attempting to identify a patient. This was the last number dialed from her cell phone."

Eyes shifting back to the soupy footage, Moira caught her breath but her stomach betrayed her and fell. Edge on edge, the cars looked like toppled dominoes on the black, shiny pavement. She sunk into the chair, searching for a familiar SUV in the murky light.

"Hello?"

Moira cleared her throat. "Yes, I'm here."

The caller went on to say that the Jane Doe was in her late twenties with light hair and a slim build. She'd been pulled from her vehicle with only a cell phone on her person.

"The call was placed yesterday. Can you or anyone else at this number give us any information?"

Moira was shaking now and the block of ice in her stomach was expanding upward, threatening to choke her. "What's the patient's condition?"

"She's stable, but unconscious. That's all I can tell you. Unless you're next of kin, of course."

After a moment of silent thanks, Moira swallowed hard and managed, "I suppose I am." She patted the desk, hunting for a pen under the rubble. "Where do I need to go?"

"You can come here, to San Francisco Memorial. I need to ask you some questions first, though. Patient's name, address and date of birth? Any distinguishing attributes, like scars or tattoos?"

Moira rapid-fire answered the first three questions and after a moment of consideration added, "Lindsay had an appendectomy when she was a kid. There's a scar below her belly button."

"Yes, that's noted here. This appears to be Ms. Foster. Was she here on business or pleasure? Is there anyone in San Francisco we should contact?"

Moira put an overwrought hand to her forehead and closed her eyes. "I'll take care of it. Thanks for the call. I'll be there in a few hours." She provided her name and cell number in case of a change in Lindsay's condition and disconnected. "Please, God. Let her be okay," she prayed, leaning back in the chair with a crunch. "What the—" She ran a hand over the leather, looking for the source of the sound. "Where the hell did you come from?" She laughed through the tears that filled her eyes. The green shards were smooth, with soft edges, like the other pieces she'd found that day. It had been a beer bottle, they'd decided. Guessing what the sea glass had been was almost as fun as making the makeshift bracelets that still occupied Moira's jewelry box. Caressing it with her thumb, she closed her eyes and made a wish.

*****

What seemed like a lifetime later, but was actually only a few hours, that wish came true.

"Ms. Brody?" asked a white-haired man wearing a lab coat over blue scrubs.

Nodding in acknowledgement, Moira rose from what upon her arrival had been the only empty chair in the waiting room.

"I'm Dr. Sorenson," he said in a businesslike tone and offered his hand.

Taking it, she introduced herself. "Moira Brody."

"Let's step over here," he suggested, gesturing off to the side.

Moira obliged, inquiring, "How is she?"

"Ms. Foster is in Recovery. She's doing well."

"Thank God."

"She has a concussion, some contusions. Lost her spleen." He consulted the iPad in his hand. "Unfortunately, we weren't able to save the baby."

"The *baby*?" Moira amazed, feeling her jaw drop.

"A D&C is unusual in the first trimester," he continued briskly, "but I thought it best under the circumstances."

"A D&C?"

He looked over the rimless glasses perched on his nose, explaining, "Dilation and Curettage. The impact from the accident likely caused the miscarriage, but we can't be sure."

"Lindsay was pregnant?"

Dr. Sorenson whipped off the glasses and gave her a puzzled look. "Being next of kin, I assumed you knew."

Still wrestling with the revelation, Moira stared at the now leery eyes narrowed on her. "No, I didn't. How far along was she?"

"It's hard to say for certain. Six to eight weeks maybe."

Moira did some quick mental math. No wonder Lindsay had called off the wedding.

"The next few hours will be telling, but Ms. Foster should make a full recovery."

"When can I see her?"

"She should be cognizant and in a room within the hour. We'll let you know." She watched his fingertips make chicken scratch-like noises on the tablet before sliding it into the pocket of his white coat and extending his hand again. "It was nice to meet you." With a tight nod, he took his leave out of the waiting room and down the hallway.

How could Lindsay not have told her? The same way she hadn't shared her feelings for Paul, she reminded herself. No, this was different. After a few seconds of debate, Moira started running. "Doctor?"

Turning on his heel, he answered tersely, as if he'd already checked her off his mental to-do list. "Yes?"

"Is it possible Ms. Foster didn't know she was pregnant?"

"That's always that possibility, of course," he replied, bottom lip pouting in consideration. "This early on some women don't realize they've conceived, especially if it was unintentional."

"I'm sure it was."

"Either way, Ms. Foster should know this won't affect her fertility. In a few months she can try again if she so desires."

Moira watched him walk away, then searched her purse for her phone, finding Lindsay's instead. The screen indicated five missed calls, all from Brian. Now Moira was even more confused. Lindsay had been leaving San Francisco when the accident happened. Had Brian not welcomed her with open arms? Then reconsidered? Had she somehow missed him? Filled with more questions then answers, Moira headed back to the waiting room.

*****

Brian hated hospitals. He still had memories of visiting his mother in one as a young boy. Apart from Kelsey's birth, he had been able to avoid them ever since. Nothing had changed; the shiny, speckled linoleum floors, the stale smell of disinfectant and the cheerless atmosphere still turned his stomach. The accident on the Bay Bridge had made the L.A. news, but he'd thought little of it once Jan confirmed no one from the firm had been involved. But that apathy had been short-lived.

What the hell was Lindsay doing in San Francisco?

He'd cut his time at USC short and headed for Tahoe after his conversation with Laura, but couldn't get a direct flight. A blessing of sorts because he was at SFO when informed by an unfamiliar voice that a woman had been admitted to San Francisco Memorial Hospital with only this cell phone on her person. The same cell phone he had been calling in vain for hours. She was tentatively identified as Lindsay Foster of Incline Village, Nevada. Next of kin was en route. The hospital was not at liberty to disclose any further information.

Running through the automatic double doors, he was greeted by a woman wearing a red smock and a sappy smile sitting behind a circular reception desk.

"Can I help you, sir?"

"I'm looking for a patient," Brian panted. "Lindsay Foster, brought in last night."

The silver-haired woman began striking the antiquated keyboard, one lazy character at a time. "Are you her husband?"

His heart surely split in two in his chest. Brian cleared his throat. "No. I'm... a friend."

The woman gave him an odd look, as if that didn't make sense. "Ms. Foster is being moved to a room. You can go to the waiting area on the fourth floor. I'll need a form of identification."

Digging his wallet out of his back pocket, Brian complied. He watched the woman run his driver's license through a keypad machine which produced a duplicate image in sticker form.

"Please wear this visibly at all times. Visiting hours end at 8:00 p.m.," she informed him, handing over his license and the badge. "The elevators are right over there."

Punching the sticker on his chest, Brian headed in the direction indicated. Married or not, Lindsay was alive.

CHAPTER NINETEEN

"LINDSAY?" THE DISTANT VOICE was comforting, familiar. Someone was coming into blurry focus, but Lindsay couldn't tell who it was. Or where she was. The lights were jewel-bright and her head hurt too much to open her eyes any further. Amid the indistinct sounds and steady beep of machines, someone was touching her arm, pressing against the inside of her wrist. After a few seconds a hand wrapped around each of her ankles, then released. Inherent fear sprung up inside her, jarring her eyes open. She was laying on a hospital bed. A woman in blue pajamas was standing over her, tapping her finger on a liquid-filled bag hanging above her head. "Linds?" The voice repeated, more hopeful this time.

Lindsay blinked away the silt that had formed on the inside of her eyes and turned her head toward the voice.

Moira's smile was warm and guarded. "There she is." She entwined their hands and the smile widened. "How do you feel? Are you in pain?"

"A little." Lindsay started to sit up, but immediately reconsidered. Her abdomen was filled with pins. "My stomach, my side."

"That's to be expected. Anywhere else?"

"My head. I was in an accident, wasn't I?"

"You and about thirty other people. On the Bay Bridge. Do you remember?"

Nodding slowly in recollection, Lindsay shifted her gaze from Moira to the only window in the room, hidden behind beige plastic blinds. The bumper-to-bumper traffic, the dense fog, the car that suddenly appeared in front of her. And the reason she was on the Bay Bridge to begin with. Tears welled in her eyes as dread coiled in her stomach. "I thought there was room ahead, but the fog was so thick."

"You rear-ended the car in front of you and were subsequently hit from behind. It was a chain reaction accident. That side of the bridge just re-opened this afternoon."

"This afternoon? What day is it?"

"It's Friday night."

"Friday night!" she flabbergasted, returning to Moira.

Moira affirmed with a nod. "Your cell was all that checked in with you. I was your last call. Got a speeding ticket outside Auburn trying to get here." Her eyes began to shine with humor. "You owe me two hundred bucks."

Lindsay squeezed the hand that held hers. What would she do without Moira?

"You lost your spleen and are a little banged up," her friend explained. Then she bit her bottom lip as if wavering between one thought and another. "And —"

"Knock, knock." A voice called from behind the door just before it whooshed open and Paul walked in. He greeted Moira with a supportive hug, then walked over to the bed and kissed Lindsay on the cheek. "Hey." His voice softened a few notches. "You gave us quite a scare." He pulled up a chair next to the bed. "How are you feeling?"

His eyes were unbelievably full and kind. Even after everything, he was here for her. What a fool she'd been. "Okay… Paul, you're here," she awed.

"Of course I'm here."

"But…"

He shook his head from side to side, then pressed his forefinger to her lips. "We can talk about all of that later. I'm just sorry it took me so long to get here."

Lindsay shifted her eyes to Moira. How had she missed the twinkle in her eyes and the pink that flashed into her cheeks before? "You guys didn't come together?"

"No!" Moira exclaimed.

Paul threw her a peculiar look, then returned to Lindsay. "I was in Portland. Jumped on the first flight out after Moira called."

"Oh, here." Moira scooped her purse off the floor and rummaged through it. "I have your phone." Her tone was oddly deliberate, almost encrypted. "You have some missed calls."

Lindsay started to reach for it, but the pain in her side was too great. "Just put it there." She pointed to the bedside table. "You were saying?" Her fingertips found the bandage above her eyebrow. "I'm a little banged up, lost my spleen and what else?"

Moira looked away, scanning the room and biting her lip. Then her indecisive gaze cut between Paul and Lindsay. Settling on Lindsay, she let out a deep breath. "Nothing. Nothing that can't wait. You need to get some rest."

*****

Brian was blowing out an overdue breath when the elevator doors opened. Seeing Moira Brody standing on the other side of them had him choking on it. Clearly surprised, her face paled, then fell. Her lips parted, formed syllables, but his name went unuttered. The control panel beeped, reminding Brian to step out. But for him to do that, Moira had to step aside. She did and finally whispering his name, wrapped her arms around him. He reciprocated as some of the day's tension rolled down his back like sweat.

Then he realized she was crying.

His arms fell automatically to his sides, releasing her. He took in the shadows under her eyes, the worry in them. His blood ran cold, and the cavity where his heart used to be emptied, leaving him hollow. Suddenly boneless, he propped himself against the stark white wall, fighting for equilibrium and air.

Until Moira smiled through her tears and assured him, "She's going to be fine."

He could do nothing but stare at her as confusion replaced the distress in her eyes. She glanced over her shoulder furtively before grabbing his arm and leading him down the hall away from the waiting room area. She studied him for a long moment, then shook her head, saying, "I don't know why I'm so happy to see you. I might be furious with you. And it only complicates things."

His suspicions had been right, he accepted with a sinking stomach. "I know."

"You *know*?"

"They told me downstairs. I don't care about that. I just want to see her. Then I'll leave."

Her expression collapsed, and the confusion was replaced with indignation and wonder. Her shoulders straightened and her mouth tightened. "Like hell you will! As if Lindsay hasn't been through enough, you walk out on her, leave her to fend for herself!"

"She left me, remember?" He began to pace, raking his fingers through his hair. "Twice. Besides, she's got Webster to take care of her. What was she doing in San Francisco anyway?"

Moira gawked at him, then answered by way of a question. "You didn't see her? She didn't tell you? About any of it?" Hands on hips, she took a few steps to the side, then back again. "Brian, what is it that you think you know?" She let her hands slap her thighs in frustration.

"Yes, do tell," a deep voice taunted. "Then it'll be my turn. Bet I know something you don't know."

Brian's innards began to boil and he could feel the heat surge through his body, then settle in his cheeks. Turning around, he narrowed his eyes and seethed, "I know that I came here to see Lindsay. And that's what I'm going to do."

Webster made a tsking sound with his tongue. "Look who took time out of his busy life to come to Lindsay's side. Day late and a dollar short, though," he barreled on, approaching Brian cavalierly. "Thankfully she's going to be all right." The other man's eyes, full of arrogance, sliced between the two of them. "Too bad about the baby, though."

Baby? Brian, frozen in the inertia of shock, lost his breath.

"Oh, didn't Lindsay share the happy news with you? What a shame." Webster, aiming a smarmy smile at Brian, went on derisively, "Now we'll never be sure whose baby it was, will we?"

A horrified gasp escaped Moira's throat as her hand flew over her mouth. "Paul, no!"

"No worries, Moirs. Lindsay and I can make more," Webster jeered, not sparing her a glance. "Obviously this isn't news to Moira." He jabbed his finger in the air a few inches from Brian's face. "So, I guess that makes you the last to know."

"I'll tell you what I know." Brian clenched his right fist, leaving one hand free to grab the other man's collar. "I know that if there was a baby, there'd be no doubt in my mind whose it would be," he hissed through his teeth. "You never got that lucky."

"I wouldn't be so sure about that," Webster roiled, challenge shining in his eyes.

"I would," Brian assured him and went for it. Webster dodged a direct hit to the mouth, turning his head just in time for Brian's knuckles to skirt his left eye. He charged back, attempting to return the favor, but Brian thwarted the fist and Webster only grazed his temple. Brian stepped back, both fists clenched this time, glaring at Webster with conspicuous ire. "You wanna go?"

Before Webster could answer, Moira flew in between them. "Stop it! Both of you! This isn't about you and your egos. This is about Lindsay." She threw her glance in the direction of quickly approaching footfalls. Then, pressing a palm to Paul's heaving chest, ordered, "You're going to step over there and cool off." She nodded toward the opposite side of the hallway, then turned to Brian. "And you're coming with me." She shifted her gaze to the man dressed in dark pants and a white shirt covered with patches who was closing in on them. "Providing I can keep the two of you from getting thrown out of here, that is."

CHAPTER TWENTY

W AKING UP ALONE THIS time, Lindsay got her bearings and scanned the room. Besides the bed in the center, there were two vinyl arm chairs trimmed in faux wood. One bedside and one under a TV mounted in the corner. There was also an overbed table on wheels. And on it, even in the dim light, she found what she was looking for. She sat up gingerly, biting back the pain radiating from her abdomen, up her side and around to her back and neck. Stretching in spite of it, she reached for the edge of the high table. Successful on the second try, she wheeled it toward her, cursing under her breath when the phone crashed to the floor. Frustrated but determined, she threw the covers aside and saw blood. Brown for the most part, it dotted the front of the hospital gown and the bed sheet below. Lindsay peeked down the loose-fitting collar of the gown. Great. On top of it all, she'd gotten her period. That would have to be tended to later. It appeared to be under control for now. She dangled her feet over the side of the bed and then one at a time, stepped onto the cold floor. Encouraged by her small accomplishment, she pushed herself up and spotting the phone just under the rail, coaxed it out with her toes. Then she braced herself against the bed with one hand and reached down for it with the other.

"What the hell do you think you're doing?"

The scornful voice startled Lindsay, making her lose her balance and tip forward. She ended up on her hands and knees next to the bed. "Shit!"

Moira was at her side within seconds, hair falling from a neglected ponytail and eyes holding the weight of the world. "What's wrong with you? You're barely out of surgery."

"I'm trying to get my phone!" Lindsay winced, catching her breath. "There isn't even a clock in this damn place."

Moira lifted her gaze to the table and then back to the floor. She cocked her head and retrieved the phone without moving an inch. "There. Anything else?"

Feeling like a scolded child, Lindsay shook her head. "No, Mother."

"Back to bed then," she ordered, standing and arranging the covers. "You look positively exhausted."

"I could say the same about you," Lindsay replied, obliging.

"It's been a long day." She paused, then added, "And babysitting takes a lot out of you."

"Babysitting?" Confused, Lindsay watched Moira cross the room and open the door.

"Yes, boys will be boys no matter how old they get. In fact, I brought one of them with me," she informed Lindsay, her voice softening. "Since he belongs to you."

Brian was standing there, framed by the glaring lights of the hallway. His hair was disheveled and he was wearing a red USC sweatshirt and wrinkled jeans. He looked at her through eyes full of regret and longing.

Her heart galloped in her chest and she could sense a smile rounding her cheeks. She felt his name whisper across her lips and wondered if that was why his expression suddenly lightened. He came toward her as fresh tears built in her throat. With a gulp, she managed, "No, he doesn't."

"He wants to." His tone was gentle, yet commanding. He didn't take his eyes off her to bid Moira goodbye or take the final strides to reach her. He simply sat on the edge of the bed and without a word, cradled her in his arms.

Lindsay collapsed into him, feeling his breath catch with hers, his heart beat accordingly. Then she realized he was crying too. She had never seen him cry; never thought it possible.

"I love you, Lindsay. I just want you to know how much I love you."

She pried herself away from him, searching his bleary eyes in wonder. "You do?"

"More than you could ever know. More than I knew, too." He brushed a hand across her slippery cheek. "I was on my way to tell you that when I heard about the accident. At first I didn't know if..." He looked away. "Damn it, Linds, I couldn't bear it if anything happened to you. Married is one thing. But if you'd—"

"Brian, I'm not—" she interrupted.

"No, let me get this out." He stood and began blazing a trail in front of the bed in the small room. "I've been so stubborn, so selfish."

She followed him with her eyes. "Me too."

"I thought I lost you. Really lost you."

"You didn't."

He stopped pacing. "I don't just mean that way."

"Neither do I. I broke off the engagement."

"I know. Moira told me." He sat again, took a recuperative breath. "She also said you were coming to see me." He smiled and took her hands in his. "So why were you leaving San Francisco?"

She shook her head, pushing away the memory. This rollercoaster of emotions was as exhausting as her injuries. "I had to. I had to get out of there after I saw you with that woman."

Brian's face went blank, not with the guilt she expected, but with bewilderment. "You saw me? Where? With what woman?"

"At the Fairmont. With a well-endowed blonde with endless legs and a very friendly disposition," Lindsay went on. "It was awful to see you with her, touching her, kissing her."

"I wasn't *with* her." Shaking his head from side to side, he seemed to debate, then decide against explaining further. "And you didn't say anything? You just left?"

"What else could I do?" Her voice jumped a little. "I was devastated. I figured you went upstairs with her."

"I didn't," he corrected her sharply.

Lindsay couldn't believe how happy that made her. "You would have had every right to."

He didn't argue the point, just asked, "Why were you at the Fairmont to begin with?"

She sensed that he already knew and that kindled the hope surging inside her, giving her the courage to go on. "I realized you're all that matters. I figured if the room was still there, waiting for me, you might be too."

That seemed to please him immensely. "What about Webster?"

Trembling, she reached out to him. "How could I possibly marry him when I'm so desperately in love with you?"

"How could I let you?" Brian fathomed. He brushed her lips with his, then began again. "What you saw was me running into an old friend. One to whom I could have easily availed myself. But even having no idea you were there, had reconsidered, I didn't. Because I didn't want to. You were the last woman in my bed. The only woman I want in my bed. Do you understand?"

Lindsay could do nothing but nod as he looked at her uncompromisingly. She tried to put her arms around him, to draw him nearer. But her side got the better of her and she flinched.

Frown lines filled his forehead. "What is it?"

"I'm just so sore. Everywhere."

"Lay back." Brian eased her back on the stacked pillows. Then he stood. "I'll have the nurse get you something for the pain."

"No," Lindsay refused, grabbing his arm. "It'll knock me out again. I want to be with you, not sleep."

He considered her for a long moment before sitting again, in the chair next to the bed this time, as if to create distance between them. Bringing her hands to his mouth, he kissed one and then the other before wrapping them in his. Trying to ignore the reservation that had crept into his eyes, she noted the bruise at the top of his cheekbone. She wiggled one hand free and explored it with her fingertip.

"What's this? It looks fresh."

"That," Brian said uneasily, "is what I have to talk to you about."

*****

Moira said the words would come. She was wrong. But tongue tangling in his mouth, Brian somehow spit them out.

"Pregnant?" Lindsay amazed. "How could I be pregnant?"

He couldn't help but chuckle at the innocence in her voice. "Well, I think I had something to do with it. Hope so anyway."

He watched her do the mental math, then lift her eyes to his. They looked impossibly blue amid the purple bruise around her eye and the red scratches on her forehead. "I couldn't have been more than…" Her voice trailed off as a tear rolled down each cheek.

"Couple months, give or take." He swallowed hard. "You didn't know?"

She shook her head and looked away. "No."

Brian relaxed a little. "I'm so sorry, Linds. The good news is that no internal damage was done. There's nothing to prevent you from getting pregnant again." Nothing but loving him, he reminded himself with an internal kick, wondering if she was thinking the same thing.

"I'm the one who should be sorry. It's been so long since I've had to worry about all that," she told him, her gaze returning to him.

Brian was appalled, "Sorry? Why should you be sorry?" He stood to pace, running a restless hand through his hair. "Lindsay, I love you. I want you." Forever, if you'll have me, he silently prayed. "How could you think you'd have to apologize for being pregnant?"

"I know your future plans don't include another child. I—"

Guilt replaced the agitation in his gut. He bolted to her side and cupped her face in his hands. "You are my future. Do you understand?"

She nodded solemnly and gave him a watery smile as the shock in her eyes turned to grief. A grief he'd caused. If he'd come to his senses earlier, she wouldn't have been on that bridge to begin with. He could see the wheels turning in her head, connecting the dots. After a long moment she asked, "But what does that have to do with the bruise?"

God, he wanted to skip that part. Fast forward to now, to concentrating on getting her out of here and healed. But she deserved to know and he had to sure. "That came from your former fiancé." Brian bit off the word. "It was an attempt to retaliate for the punch I threw him. An automatic reaction on my part after he announced that you'd just miscarried his baby."

Her brows knitted together as her eyes narrowed. "*His* baby? But Paul knows the baby couldn't have been his!"

Brian felt his heart resume its regular rhythm. He let out a sigh of relief. "That's what I hoped you'd say."

She gave him a confused look. "Hoped?"

"You were engaged, married for all I knew. I didn't know how far along you were. A lot can change in two months."

"That never changed."

"Then what did?"

"Everything, nothing. I couldn't live without you, Brian," she croaked. "I tried, but I couldn't. And then I thought it was too late."

Crooning her name, he took her in his arms. "I'm sorry. I'm so sorry. It doesn't matter now anyway."

"It does matter. I want to talk about it." She pushed a little away from him. "It was the bracelet."

Brian searched his memory. "The diamond one I gave you for Christmas? Moira has it."

She brought an alarmed hand to her chest and exhaled deeply. "Oh! I'd forgotten I was wearing it. But I'm talking about the sea glass bracelet. Like the ones Moira and I used to make when we were kids."

"Okay," he said slowly, nesting her hands into the curve of his.

"A few days ago Moira and I were at the beach," Lindsay started again. "She collected some sea glass and decided to make a bracelet. But she miscalculated the number of pieces she'd found and cut the wire too long."

Brian wondered what this had to do with anything. "All right."

"Turns out she didn't miscalculate, she dropped a piece. I found it later when I was taking out the trash and threw it in her purse. I didn't realize she'd made the bracelet for me until after she left."

Brian could only nod, struggling a bit to keep up.

"The next day I went to the cemetery. I sat there for a long time, thinking, crying, asking Gram for advice. I knew I had to break off the engagement. But I still didn't know why. Not really, anyway. It was a chilly morning; I grabbed a sweater from the car. When I reached into the pocket, I found a piece of sea glass."

"A different piece?"

"Yeah," she confirmed. "After Gram died, I'd wander the beach for hours, trying to clear my head. I must have picked it up and forgotten about it. It was nothing like the shards Moira had found the day before. This one was weathered, jagged, sharp."

Her voice was hoarse, her expression taxed, but she seemed determined to make her point, so Brian resisted the urge to take her back in his arms. Instead he shook his head in encouragement.

"After I broke off the engagement, I walked on the beach for a while and ended up at Hues of Blue. Mac was working. He recounted your conversation." Sitting up without wincing this time, she lightened a little and went on, "When I pulled out my wallet, the sea glass surfaced again. I was mesmerized by it, felt compelled to do something with it. So right there at the bar, I unwound the wire on the bracelet Moira had made. There was just enough slack to attach the old piece. It looked out of place at first; it was bigger, thicker, rougher around the edges. I never would have thought to put it with the others, but it became the focal point of the bracelet and fit my wrist perfectly."

"Then it hit me. I had that missing piece all along, but didn't add it to the rest because I thought it wouldn't fit. I thought everything had to be perfect, just the way I'd planned or not at all. I assumed that I could use, force really, another presumably flawless piece to finish the bracelet. But I was wrong; it was merely a placeholder." Her eyes began to shimmer as she rested a hand on his cheek. "Until I found you again. You're the missing piece, Brian. The only one that fits."

*****

Moira walked into the converted closet serving as a security office on the ground floor of the hospital and prepared for battle. "Hey, Cowboy."

Paul looked up and shot her a weary smile. "Hey."

"May I?" she asked, pointing to the empty chair beside him.

"Sure."

"How's the shiner?"

He removed the ice pack and blinked a few times. "Better than my pride. Rembrandt has a helluva of a right hook."

"You held your own. I'm just glad you're still speaking to me."

"The alternative wasn't a viable option. You're my ride home."

She laughed in spite of herself. "I'm sorry, Paul. About everything. And calling you was a knee-jerk reaction. I should have thought it through. "

It surprised her that the eyes that held hers were filled with relief and understanding, not pain and resentment. "You know what? I'm not. It's exhausting trying to make a love affair out of a friendship. We tried so hard to make it work, both wanted it to so desperately, but it just wasn't there. Down deep, I was always waiting for the other shoe to drop. Now that it has, we can stop pretending. Lindsay was right; we love each other, but we aren't in love with each other. Neither one of us wanted to accept that. Especially me."

Moira was still processing his conciliatory words, almost afraid to believe them, when the security guard returned. "Mr. Webster, you're free to go. No charges will be filed since no property damage was done. But please, take it outside next time. Or better yet, buy each other a beer and bury the hatchet." He handed Paul a clipboard with a pen attached. "Sign the top sheet. The bottom copy is yours."

Paul stood and followed the directions. "Thanks."

Then the paunchy man addressed Moira. "Keep an eye on him, Miss."

"I'll try."

They walked down the hallway toward the exit. After a dozen strides of companionable silence, Paul said, "I guess I owe Lindsay an apology."

"Probably." Then Moira decided to pose the question that had been eating at her. "How in the world did you know? *I* didn't even know. *She* didn't even know."

Paul tossed her a facetious grin. "Chatty floor nurse. She assumed I was the baby's father. I didn't tell her otherwise." Then his gaze clouded and his tone softened. "How'd she take it?"

"I let Brian tell her."

Paul thought about that and nodding admitted, "I guess I was mad, hurt."

"I know."

He stopped walking and stared at her as if he'd never seen her before. "You really do, don't you, Moirs? You always understand."

Her heartbeat cantered, then leveled, becoming butterflies in her stomach. "I love her too, you know."

"I know." Nodding, Paul took a few steps forward, activating the floor sensors and opening the double doors to the sounds of the city. Then he tuned back to her. "I also know that I'm starving. Want to get something to eat before we hit the

175

road? You still owe me that rain check, you know," he added playfully.

Feeling lighter than she had in months, Moira couldn't think of any reason why not.

CHAPTER TWENTY-ONE

"OKAY, EASY NOW," BRIAN said three days later, coaxing Lindsay to the couch in her living room. He sat down next to her, brought her legs across his lap and removed her shoes.

"I can't believe I'm so tired from doing nothing."

"That's normal after surgery. Plus you had a miscarriage. Your body is using all of its energy to heal."

He rubbed her calves, then rose and spread the throw from the back of the couch over her. "I'll unload the car and make you something to eat. Do you have any soup?"

Lindsay smiled up at him. He'd hardly left her side at the hospital. She'd had to threaten checking herself out for him to go home to get some decent sleep the night before. "I think there's some in there. I'll be fine. You need to get going. You're not used to those mountain roads at night."

He gave her an odd look and then crouching down beside her, declared flatly, "I'm not going anywhere. Do you really think I'd leave you alone like this?"

"Surely you must have to get back to work. You've been gone for nearly a week including your truncated trip to USC. What about the All Tech case?"

"Jan has been keeping me in the loop. I have a meeting with their CEO in the morning. He has a home here, remember?"

"Is Mike keeping an eye on your apartment?"

"I guess."

"You guess?"

"My alarm is monitored. Besides, I'm not going home without you," Brian promised, stroking the side of her face with his fingers.

"You're not?" Lindsay was floored.

"No," he answered, as if the question was outrageous. "I'm not going home until you're strong enough to come with me." His expression fell a little. "I thought you wanted that too."

"I do," she told him. "It's just that we never really talked about it."

He chewed on that a bit, then sitting on the edge of the couch, spoke in a quiet voice. "No, we haven't. But more importantly, we haven't talked about losing our baby."

And that was not by chance. Lindsay had avoided bringing it up and managed to change the subject whenever Brian had. "I don't know what there is to say. The social worker in the hospital said to expect feelings of denial, waves of grief, maybe even depression. But I don't feel any of that. I'm numb. Maybe it's the pain pills. Or maybe it's because I didn't know I was pregnant."

"I know what you mean. I've been so worried about you, I haven't given much thought to the baby." He played with the ends of her hair. "But I have been thinking about your suitcase."

"My suitcase?"

"It was full. Were you were planning to stay for a while?"

"I hoped so. I thought about going to your place, asking Mike to let me in, get a read from him."

"A read?"

"He would have known if you were seeing someone, had moved on. Going to the hotel was safer, less humbling." She paused, then added, "Or so I thought."

"He would have told you I wasn't, hadn't." He tilted her face to his and looked her square in the eye. "Linds, before we go any farther, I have to know you're not going to run away again."

She shook her head from side to side in unequivocal confirmation. "I couldn't if I wanted to. I'm sorry you had to ask." She gave him a sheepish smile. "So would you have liked to come home and find me in your apartment with my suitcase unpacked?"

"Sure. Especially if you were naked."

"Seriously."

"I am serious," he said, his eyes dancing with humor. "In a perfect world, I would have come home and found you naked in my apartment with your suitcase unpacked."

"It's going to be a while until we can get naked together again."

"That will only make it better," he said. "I waited a year for you without even knowing it. What makes you think I wouldn't wait a little while longer?"

She shrugged off the question. "Nothing, I guess."

But Brian called her out. "That doesn't sound like nothing."

She wondered if he came by the love in his eyes honestly or if it was a reflection of her own. Or in a perfect world, both. "Did you ever doubt, even for a second, that the baby was yours?"

"Not really. But it wouldn't have mattered anyway."

"It wouldn't have?"

He shook his head from side to side categorically. "I would have still loved you, wanted you."

"Even if I was pregnant with another man's baby?" she asked, incredulous.

"I hadn't gone there yet; too cocky I guess. For all I knew you were married. It would have been a matter of you leaving Webster, baby or not."

"Down deep I knew I couldn't marry Paul. I was talking myself into it."

"Good to know. Saved me from being the ass in the back of the church."

"What?" Lindsay asked through a yawn.

"Nothing," he answered, standing. "Now go to sleep. We'll figure all of this out later."

*****

Why was Gram making soup at this hour? Lindsay mumbled to herself as the indisputable scent of chicken stock laced with sweet spice filled the air. Opening her eyes, she scanned the living room. The deck door was ajar letting in the night breeze, no doubt the vehicle for the savory aroma. Then, realizing it wasn't Gram in the kitchen, but Brian, she jolted up with a racing heart. The house was dark, lit only by the narrow light above the stove. Brian was unloading three Raley's bags perched on the kitchen counter, while speaking in a hushed tone.

"My assistant usually handles these things, but I can't reach her," he was saying into the phone. He listened for a few moments then spoke again, "Yes, SFO to DCA." There was another pause. "Yeah." He bent down and the open refrigerator door prevented Lindsay from hearing the rest of the conversation. But shortly thereafter, she heard the beep of disconnection and Brian stood and slid the phone into his pocket.

She watched him work, alternating between emptying the bags and stirring a pot on the stove. She could almost taste the soup of her childhood, full of carrots and thick noodles, celery and chunks of chicken. And that secret ingredient that made everything better, she recalled, feeling her throat tighten. She laid a hand on her stomach, still in awe that she'd been pregnant. Would she ever make such memories with a child of her own? She wiped a lone tear from the outer corner of her eye and let out an acquiescent breath.

"You're up!" Brian announced, walking to her. "I wondered if you'd just sleep through the night."

She shifted and made room for him to sit. "How long was I asleep?"

"Long enough for me to buy some groceries and an air mattress. Since you can't climb the stairs, we'll sleep down here on that tonight."

We? He was not only going to stay, but sleep downstairs with her?

"Is that okay?" He waved a hand in front of her face as if to free her from a trance.

"Of course. I just can't believe you're here. First the hospital, then bringing me home and now staying."

Sitting down, Brian settled her against him and linked his arms across her upper chest. "Why can't you believe it?"

Because she still couldn't believe this wasn't a dream. Except for losing the baby, that is. "For one thing, you're in the middle of a huge case."

"We've already discussed that."

"What about your trip?"

He stiffened. "To D.C.? How did you know about that?"

"When I woke up you were on the phone. It sounded like you were booking a flight."

"I was canceling a flight. The environmental lobbyists aren't going anywhere."

"But—"

"No more buts!" He gently turned her to face him. "I'm not going to D.C. or anywhere else without you."

She gazed into his wild eyes, cautious hope churning in her stomach. "Because you feel guilty, obligated?"

"Oh, I feel guilty all right." His voice clipped. "It was my fault you were on that bridge, my fault you lost your baby, my fault you didn't know how much I love you. Because I didn't know it myself. I've never loved anyone like this before, needed anyone like this before, almost lost them. I'm scared to death, I don't know what I'm doing, but I know I never want to go through anything like that again." He sucked in some air, then finished quietly, "But most of all, it's because I know I want to spend the rest of my life with you, if you'll have me."

Overwhelmed with joy, she rested her head in the crook of his shoulder. "I will indeed."

CHAPTER TWENTY-TWO

A WEEK LATER, MOIRA SAT on the floor of Lindsay's closet, trying on a pair of shoes.

"Are you sure you don't want these?" she asked, modeling the black espadrille.

"Positive. The toe box is too narrow, gave me a nasty blister." Running her hands through her hair, Lindsay considered the bed cluttered with clothes and lined with shoes. "I think I'm done for now. We'll get the rest next time."

"Did you decide about school?" Moira inquired, walking over to the full-length mirror.

"I'm probably going to enroll in the Berkeley Extension Art and Design Program next semester," she answered, unzipping the largest suitcase she owned.

"I'm so happy for you, Linds."

Dropping Brian's favorite lace nightgown into the bag, she watched her friend contemplate her reflection. And decided the time had come. "Why didn't you tell me?"

"Tell you what?" Moira replied lightly, turning to face her.

"About Paul. About how you felt about him." Watching Moira's face go blank, Lindsay elaborated, "How long has it been? How long have you been in love with him?"

"Don't be ridiculous." Moira's mouth was instantly tight, her tone inhospitable. "I'm not in love with Paul." She sat on the window seat and began removing the wedges.

"Yes, you are," Lindsay contended, sure for the first time. Kneeling, she settled her friend's busy hands, watching as fever spread to her checks. "You're blushing."

Heavy silence hovered over them for a long moment. Moira broke it on a sigh, "I don't know how long it's been. I wasn't sure for a long time. Hell, I'm not even sure now." Freeing her hands, she pushed herself up and began wringing them. "I might be confusing my feelings of friendship for more. We're familiar, comfortable." Her voice grew lower, a little self-deprecating. "It doesn't matter anyway. Paul would never think of me that way."

Lindsay followed Moira with her eyes as she crossed the room. "You don't know that. And neither does he. So instead of finding out, you would have let me marry him, watch us make a life together while you suffered in silence? For how long? Until it became too much to bear and I lost you too?"

"You could never lose me, you know that." She lowered her sheepish gaze. "I guess I realized things had changed when you were living in San Francisco. Paul and I found ourselves alone more than we had been in…forever. It was gradual and," she clarified hastily, "completely one-sided. Nothing ever happened."

"Why?"

"Because it's not meant to be." She waved away the notion. "My infatuation will pass."

"You don't know that. And what if it's not an infatuation?" Lindsay sent Moira a long, reflective stare. "What if you're making the biggest mistake of your life, like I almost made the biggest mistake of mine?" she proposed, standing. "You think you've never been in love. But maybe you've been in love for half your life without even knowing it."

"Yeah," she grunted sarcastically. "With someone who thinks of me as a sister. How did you—" Suddenly mortified, she interrupted herself. "Oh God! Does Paul know?"

"No."

"Then how?"

"In a roundabout way, Gram. After forcing me to be honest with myself, we moved on to you." Closing the distance between them, Lindsay forged on. "And Mrs. Donahue. Apparently she has always known. And I should have too."

"Mrs. Donahue…" Moira shook off the confusion and continued, "I know I should have told you." She dabbed the inner corners of her eyes with her fingertips. "But Grace was dying, you were heartsick and the next thing I knew Paul was looking at rings."

"That must have been awful for you."

"You'd think so, but it wasn't. So maybe it's all in my head," she said, as if trying to convince herself more than Lindsay.

"I think it's all in your heart. And around your wrist." Lindsay joined their hands and finished with an aching throat. "What did we do if there wasn't enough sea glass for two bracelets?"

"Make one and share it," Moira answered with a shrug.

"But somehow I always ended up with it," Lindsay reminded her. "You always gave it to me." She pressed the flawless piece of sea glass she'd found the night of the wedding into Moira's hand. "This time you need to keep it for yourself."

*****

Brian had hated to leave, but there was only so much he could handle from Tahoe and Jan needed his signature on a few things that couldn't be done electronically. So he'd flown out early this morning, spent a frenzied day in the office and jumped on a late afternoon flight back. And true to his word, he hadn't gone home without Lindsay. He blew out a long, slow breath. He'd made it. Almost, that is. He was coming to the curve on Lakeshore Boulevard where the lake presents itself for the first time. The water only teases at first, darting in and out from behind the massive trees before emerging, ubiquitous in all its splendor. The melted snow appears to have parted the mountains itself, having found the perfect home amid the alpenglow. And it was that pastel-drenched, fading light that Brian was chasing.

He was grateful to Moira for spending the day with Lindsay, but hoped she wouldn't stay the night. He was looking forward to enjoying what was left of the sunset over a bottle of wine. And sleeping with her nestled in his arms. But making love to her, he reminded himself begrudgingly, would have to wait a little longer.

It was the first time in a long time that he'd had somewhere to rush to after work. Where someone was waiting for him. He could get used to coming home to a house lit up like a Christmas tree instead of a dark apartment, Brian decided, throwing the car into park and stepping out into the crisp evening air. And he didn't even have to go inside to find what he was looking for. She was on the deck in a skimpy black dress and shiny heels to match. He watched her fill two wine glasses, while a ribbon of diamonds mingled with the weathered sea glass on her wrist. And his fly bulged.

Lindsay spun around, as if uncannily aware of his arrival. She sent him a subtle smile and waved in greeting. She began walking toward him, then heeded his hand with a puzzled expression. After taking in every inch of her, ingraining it in his memory, he advanced the three strides between them and took her mouth. She fell into the kiss and then hugging him tight, buried her face in his shoulder. She smelled of lilacs and garlic weaved with wine.

"You look incredible. I missed you so much," Brian told her. Need was raining down on him, soaking him to the bone. Their chests rose and fell as one in silence for a few moments as the world righted itself again. Then he broke away asking, "What's all this?"

"It's dinner. Salmon, twice baked potatoes and green beans with slivered almonds," she replied, blotting her damp lower lashes with her fingertips. "And angel food cake with strawberries for dessert."

"You did all this? In your condition?"

She nodded brightly. "How was your day?" she asked, turning back to the impeccably set table.

"Hectic," he grunted, loosening his tie.

She handed him a glass of wine, then took a sip of hers. "Don't you want to know about mine?" She shot him a bewitching look over the rim of her glass.

Intrigued, Brian shrugged. "Sure."

"I went to the doctor."

"The doctor?" Damn it, he knew he shouldn't have left. "What did he say?"

"That I'm healing nicely. And able to resume all normal activities."

She was staring at him expectantly, wide-eyed as a spring doe with the inkling of a roguish smile curving the corners of her mouth. Brian made quick work of the small space between them and laid the palms of his hands on each side of her face. "*All* activities?"

Moving her head up and down slowly, she commanded in a husky voice, "Make love to me, Brian. Like it's the first time."

She loved him, wanted him and nothing else. She was willing to give up everything she thought her life would be for him. And now she was asking him to make love to her. "Every time is like the first time with you," he proclaimed and picked her up.

She leaned into his shoulder with a soft sigh as he climbed the stairs. The bedroom was washed in dusk and smelled of her, like she'd dabbed herself on every fiber, every surface. "The last time I carried you up here and made love to you you weren't mine," he reminded her, gently setting her on the bed. "Are you mine now?"

"I've been yours since that night in Sausalito," she told him like he should have already known. "That's when I first fell in love with you."

Laying on top of her, he tightened his grip. "I feel like I fall in love with you over and over again." Her eyes were smoky in the soft light and they filled him with an indescribable aplomb. That he'd gone so long without her seemed unfathomable. "But the first night we spent together wasn't in Sausalito. It was here. The night we made love on the beach," he said, brushing her hair back from her face to take all of her in.

She smiled up at him dreamily. "I know. But we were in Sausalito when you told me you loved me for the first time."

He nodded as the memory came back to him. "The closest I'd ever come to feeling that way before was when I held Kelsey for the first time." He watched his words settle in her eyes and fill them with shimmer.

"You never told me that," she whispered, stroking the side of his face.

Because he'd only just realized it himself. "Would it have made a difference?"

She hesitated, then answered in a voice full of emotion. "I don't know. One of the reasons I left was that I didn't think you felt the same way I did. That you never would."

Her admission was bittersweet because he could see the hurt in her eyes again, like when he'd told her about the losing the baby. "Why?"

"I'd never truly loved someone before. But you had been married, had already experienced that."

"That was different. Almost like I wasn't me then." He pulled back a little and threw his gaze into the night momentarily before asking, "Do you believe that I truly love you now?"

"I want to believe it so badly it hurts."

"The last thing I want to do is hurt you," he told her. "In fact, I want to do the exact opposite."

She laughed a little. "Yes, I can feel that."

"I've never loved anyone the way I love you, Lindsay. And I never will."

The shimmer returned and intensified. "Show me."

He began with her lips, then her face and throat. She trembled beneath him as his hands skimmed her body, searching for a place to start. Sliding his hand under her, he searched for a zipper. "How the hell do I get this off?"

"The zipper is on the side," she told him, arching her back slightly and opening the dress at the same time. Underneath it was the sexiest piece of lingerie Brian had ever seen. Barely covering her breasts and torso, the black lace led to a strip of satin between her thighs. "Do you like it?" she asked from perched elbows. "I bought it just for you."

Carnal thoughts threatened all sense of decency as he eased her back down. "I'd like it a lot better on the floor. What else do you have just for me?"

"All of me is just for you," she lured, unbuttoning his shirt. "If you want me, that is."

"I've wanted you since the last time I had you. After this, I'll only want you again."

"Then take me." She slid his shirt off behind him and traced a seductive line down his chest to his waistband with her finger.

"I don't just want to take you. I want it to last all night. I want to have you over and over again." He took her mouth with his, drawing out the kiss. Then he made his way down to her earlobe, tugging at it with his teeth. "I want to make you scream for me. In the moonlight, like before."

Her head snapped up and her eyes fired with desire. "Bri," she gasped. "It's too early to go out on the beach."

"Then we'll make our own moonlight." He returned to her neck, making tiny circles with his tongue. Her moans of pleasure filled the room as his mouth made its way slowly downward.

He slid the lace down to her stomach, fully exposing her breasts. His mouth took each one, sucking, pulling, nibbling until her nipples were as hard as he could feel himself getting and she cooed beneath him. But he was nowhere near done; he wanted all of her in his mouth. He slipped two fingers inside the satin and found her. She was dripping wet. That sent a lascivious shiver through him, forced him to pause to collect himself. Her eyes were closed, her arms at her side in sublime surrender, her hair strewn across the pillow. She had never looked more beautiful. Licking his way, he unsnapped the buttons covering her dampness and spread her legs apart. Her clean-shaven triangle was as silky smooth as the passionate endearments escaping her lips. And Brian couldn't wait to taste it.

She held his head in her hands as he dove at her, digging her heels against his thighs as he explored her center, darting in and out with his tongue and fingers. He loved hearing her pant, moan, beg above him. For him. He loved feeling her grind her hips, grip the bedding for ballast, quiver as the arc of gratification built within. And most of all he loved being inside her.

But first she had to come.

Just then, as if reading his mind, she let out a long, low cry of pleasure and screaming his name, tightened her legs against him, then let herself fall. He tore himself away from her, letting his fingers continue their dance inside her as he knelt above her. He could feel her wet and throbbing against his hand. And his cock following suit.

She opened her eyes, and looking wonderfully spent, extended her arms in invitation. "I want you inside me. I want us to come together this time."

Unable to wait one moment more, Brian kicked off his pants and entered her with a deep groan of satisfaction. He was afraid to thrust too hard at first lest he hurt her. But she raised her hips in invitation to meet his and he began to rock above her. He felt her start to spasm again, drenching him and coaxing him deeper and deeper into her. Already on the edge, he muttered her name and exploded into her just as she shattered beneath him, granting her wish and knowing she was his.

CHAPTER TWENTY-THREE

"KNOCK, KNOCK."

Paul's head popped up from the drafting table. After a measured gaze, he allowed her a careful smile. "Lindsay." He rose and tucking his ruling pen above his ear, approached her beckoningly. "Come in."

Inwardly thankful for the hospitable greeting, she met him halfway across the office. "I'm sorry I didn't call first. Alex told me to come on in."

"You never have to call. You should know that. Here," he invited with outstretched hand, "have a seat."

"No, I can't stay," she refused, wondering if he could hear her heart racing.

He looked at her expectantly. "Okay."

Reaching into her purse, she handed him an octagon-shaped box. "I came by to give you this."

"Oh, yeah. That." His features instantly sobered. "I've been meaning to call you. To see how you were doing, settle some things."

"I'm sorry it's taken me so long to return it," she apologized nervously. "I wanted to come myself. I couldn't drive until yesterday."

"No problem." He stared at the box for a few moments, then began again in a businesslike tone. "The developer is buying the lot back for cash, in exchange for the drawings of the house to build as an inventory home. I'll handle all of that, since the lot is in my name."

Lindsay let out a shallow breath "Great. Thanks." Then, wringing her hands, she sputtered, "Paul, I'm so sorry. I never meant to hurt you, lead you on. I was so sad, so lonely, so unbelievably confused. And the next thing I knew I was trying on my mother's dress, buying a house, planning a wedding. I should have listened to the little voice inside my head and put a stop to it."

He shook his head in understanding. "I shouldn't have rushed you. You were vulnerable." He took a deep breath and kept going. "I'm glad you stopped by. I owe you an apology for my behavior at the hospital. I shouldn't have gotten into it with Rembrandt. I was just surprised. You told me you had feelings for him. I guess I didn't want to believe you'd acted on them."

"It wasn't like that," she hastened to inform him. "We spent one unforeseen night together and parted ways agreeing to disagree. I hadn't heard from him since." She crossed the room and searched the mountains for the words. "After it happened, I convinced myself it was the closure I needed to move on. I knew telling you would only hurt you. You still would have married me. You're too good a person not to." She turned around to face him. "But I ended up hurting you anyway." In three determined steps she closed the space between them. "I really do love you, Paul. I always will."

"I know," he replied, his face cracking into a half-smile. "I should have known all along it was too good to be true."

She took his hands, still holding the ring box, in hers. "*You're* too good to be true. That was part of the problem. I couldn't find anything wrong with you. No reason not to marry such a wonderful man. Until I realized if my feelings were insincere yours had to be too."

He gave her a baffled look. "How so?"

"If you aren't the one for me, I'm not the one for you. Which means," she felt the smile build in her heart before spreading to her mouth, "there's a very lucky girl out there, waiting for you. And I can't wait to meet her," she told him, hoping she already had.

He cocked his head and gave her a playful grin. "That's what my mom said." He paused and then laughing with his eyes, admitted, "But I figured she was biased."

Lindsay bit her lip, then lowered her gaze as her stomach sank. She had yet to speak with Paul's parents and apologize.

"She wasn't all that surprised, said she never saw any real sizzle between us," Paul went on as if clairvoyant. "More companionship, fondness, friendship. They're glad it happened sooner rather than later." His voice grew resolute. "They will always love you. And so will I."

She fell into him then, drained, as relief washed over her. He had freed her, lifted the last weight on her heart. But there was one more matter to settle. Stepping out of his embrace, she cleared her throat. "I have something else for you." Reaching into her shoulder bag, she pulled out an envelope and handed it to him. "The tickets to the hospital fundraiser. Your mom sent them to me months ago."

Paul shrugged, clearly unimpressed. "Thanks. I'll give them back to her."

"You should go. It's a great cause, always a good time."

"Naw," he said, waving the notion away. "Who would I ask on such short notice?"

"I don't know." Lindsay mocked conjecture. "How about Moira?"

"Moira?" His eyebrows rose in surprise, but his eyes began to sparkle a bit. "She'd have to get all dressed up. You know how she hates all that stuff."

"You'd be surprised. All us girls like to get dressed up once in a while. Even Moira."

"But Moira's not a date. She's..." He let his brain catch-up with his mouth. "Moira."

"She most certainly is a date," Lindsay pointed out, lifting her chin. "The best kind. You already know you'll have a good time. No awkward first date small talk."

She watched him study the tickets for longer than necessary. Then he shrugged his shoulders and said, "I'll think about it."

That, Lindsay thought with an inward cheer, is exactly what Moira had said.

CHAPTER TWENTY-FOUR

CROSSING THE BAY BRIDGE in the bright winter sunshine, Lindsay was taking in a beautiful, unobstructed view of San Francisco Bay and the Oakland Hills. "Who are we meeting again?" she asked Brian, thumbing through *Architectural Digest*.

"A friend of mine from law school. He wants to meet you and show us his new house."

"He wants to meet me?"

"Yeah. I haven't seen him in a while. He wants to catch-up."

"Okay," Lindsay replied absently, going back to the magazine.

They exited the bridge and merged into traffic on Highway 24 toward Walnut Creek. Dog-earing the article on romantic second homes, Lindsay looked up just as Brian turned off the freeway. They entered a quaint neighborhood with large houses and manicured lawns, children playing in the yards and dogs barking in the distance. Brian pulled onto a tree-lined street with a cul-de-sac at the end. Straight ahead, nestled in the trees, sat a charming two-story white brick house with slate blue shutters and window boxes bursting with pansies. "This is it," he announced, parking in the circular driveway.

"Who lives here again?" Lindsay asked, as they walked hand in hand up the winding path leading to the front door.

"You'll see," he replied, letting go of her hand.

But instead of knocking on the door, Brian took a key out of his pocket and unlocked it.

Stomach spinning with confusion and intuition, she followed the direction of his outstretched hand and stepped inside. Gleaming oak floors shone in the afternoon sunlight. Her gaze rested on the fireplace and mantle in the living room, giving her to a wistful moment. She had always wanted a masonry fireplace to hang stockings on at Christmas. Beyond the dining room she saw a Mediterranean-style kitchen with a bay window and a fenced-in backyard.

"Brian, whose house is this? It's empty," she asked, advancing a few slow steps.

"It's ours. If you want it, that is."

"Ours?" She gaped at him as the little voice inside her head got louder.

Nodding, he reached into his pocket and retrieved a small black box. Eyes locked on hers, he entwined their hands. "I love you, Lindsay. Will you be my wife? Share my life? Raise a family here with me?"

Bowled over, Lindsay looked on as he opened the velvet box. In it lay a square cut diamond, at least two carats in size, set on a thick platinum band.

"I thought the setting suited you. Simple, yet elegant; beautiful, without being ostentatious." He removed the ring and slid it on her left hand as she continued to stare at him in astonishment. "Well, what do you think?"

Lindsay shifted her gaze downward. The sunlight danced off the diamond, bringing out every color of the rainbow. She had dreamed of this moment for as long as she could remember and now it was real. And better than she could have ever imagined. Tearing her eyes away from the ring, she cupped his face in her hands. "It's incredible. But Brian, you don't have to do this. You're enough for me. I know that now. Besides, you've done all that before."

"I haven't done it with you," he told her, grasping her wrists. "And I didn't really do it, not all the way at least. Mine was kind of an abbreviated version. I didn't think I ever wanted to.

But I do, as long as it's with you." The cadence of his voice sped up as he continued, "If you don't like the house, we can sell it. There were other bidders. It's just that Moira and I both thought—"

"Moira?" Lindsay interrupted, taking a step backward. "She knows about this? She can't keep a secret for her life." Not this kind anyway, she reminded herself.

"Well, she kept this one. She flew in for a power day of house hunting. There were other houses on our short list if this one doesn't work. She thought you'd especially like the yard and the fireplace. I figured the East Bay would be the best choice," he explained, taking a recuperative breath. "It's convenient for me to work and school for you. Danville has great schools and is a very family-oriented community. We'll keep my apartment, in case we want to stay in the city or I have a late night. We can continue living there for now if you want to change some things in the house. I'm sure it's not as contemporary as you'd like."

Lindsay couldn't speak; she was simply overwhelmed with joy. She'd chosen the man over the dream. Could she really have it all?

"Linds, I'm getting a little nervous here. Put me out of my misery and give me an answer. I'm most concerned about the proposal. You can take your time on the house."

She jumped into his arms. "The answer is yes! Yes, yes, yes, yes!" she exclaimed, showering his face with kisses. "Of course to the proposal. And to the house. It's perfect. I don't want to change a thing. I didn't think I could be any happier than I was, but I was wrong."

"Thank God. When you didn't say anything, my mind started racing."

"I was in shock. I still am. I can't believe this is happening." She looked down at the future, bright as the Tahoe sunshine, resplendent on her finger. "I love you, Brian. You're all my dreams come true. And so much more."

"I love you too," he said, taking her in his arms for a proper kiss. "You're the dream I never knew I had come true."

Tears brimming her eyes, she twisted the bracelet on her wrist as he held her close. And with nothing to wish for, gave thanks instead.

The End

Read on for a sneak peek of *Chance Encounter*, the second installment in the *Chances Trilogy* by Martha O'Sullivan

CHAPTER ONE

IT HAD BEEN AGES since Delaney Richards had given a man a second thought, let alone a second look. But the pilot with the hints of gray at the temples of his chestnut-colored hair and smiling eyes had caught her unwitting attention. She watched him greet the oncoming passengers before his gaze found hers and lingered. Then, fever rushing to her cheeks, she pretended to contemplate the baggage handlers loading an adjacent plane. She felt his measured stare for a moment more before he turned away.

"Can I bring you a drink before takeoff?"

Delaney shifted her attention in the direction of the hospitable voice. "Water, please," she told the woman standing over her left shoulder. "Maybe a glass of red wine after takeoff."

The flight attendant shook her head in acknowledgement. "The aisle seat in your row isn't booked. Make yourself comfortable."

Delaney watched her return to the front of the plane and whisper something to the pilot. Nodding in affirmation, he began retreating into the cockpit, but stopped short. His amber eyes met Delaney's and held briefly before he closed the door.

Shaking off the revery, Delaney opened her bag and retrieved her laptop. Being appointed interim vice-president had been a well-deserved yet unexpected promotion. And as luck would have it, she'd been thrown out of the frying pan and into the fire. Rebranding an investment firm with a reputation for tolerating sexual harassment in today's unsparing business climate had been a challenge to say the least. It had consumed her life for the last few months. Her presentation in San Francisco next week could ensure the position became permanent. And she planned to nail it.

She had no sooner brought up the opening slide of her PowerPoint presentation when the flight crew asked for everyone's attention to review the safety procedures. Like most of the passengers, Delaney immediately tuned them out. Until a resounding voice filled the cabin, abruptly pulling her out of work mode.

"Welcome to United Airlines Flight 1126 to San Francisco. This is your captain. We anticipate a smooth four-hour-and-change flight to SFO this evening. I'll update you along the way about our progress as well as point out any landmarks of note below. Thanks for flying with us. Enjoy the flight. We've got the best crew in the business with us tonight."

The next thing she knew, the flight attendant was back at her elbow again. "Not only do you have your row to yourself, but we've got the good

California wine tonight." She handed Delaney a glass and a cocktail napkin. "This must be your lucky day."

Delaney returned the smile as the other woman took her leave. Maybe it was. Maybe her luck was finally starting to change.

*****

Even after twenty-plus years behind the stick Captain Mike Savoy never took a smooth landing for granted. Technical check behind him, he exchanged pleasantries with the flight crew before going out into the cabin to thank the passengers for their business. But tonight his motivation was admittedly twofold. He wanted to see the woman in first-class again. She'd been asleep when he'd left the cockpit mid-flight, and he'd surprised himself by pausing to study her. He hadn't seen her on the countless Chicago to San Francisco flights he'd commanded in the last few years.

"Joining us for dinner, Mike?"

He reluctantly shifted his gaze from the brunette to the blonde staring at him hopefully. Shaking his head, he gave her a closemouthed smile. "Not tonight. I've got some paperwork to catch-up on before I'm out of here."

"I'll wait for you, have a drink until you're done."

Mike sensed the innuendo in the voice of the woman almost young enough to be his daughter. He had a strict no mixing business with pleasure policy. And Caitlin would definitely be pleasure. "You guys go on," he told her. "Maybe next time."

"All right." He felt Caitlin's eyes trail his to the only remaining passenger in the first-class cabin. "You have my cell in case you change your mind." She stepped aside, allowing the cleaning crew to enter before lifting the handle of her wheeled bag. "Good night."

"Good night," Mike threw over his shoulder. The woman had flawless olive skin and her lips shimmered with the same shade of pink gloss that glazed her fingernails. Holding the phone in the crook of her shoulder, she was writing furiously on an envelope. He looked on as she disconnected, then slipped the phone into her enormous purse and stood. Mike nearly tripped over his feet trying to reach her before she slid her carry-on out of the overhead compartment.

"Let me get that." Reaching over her head, he grabbed the bag. It was heavier than he expected. "Long trip?"

"Just a week or so," she answered with a bright smile. "I've been through the lost luggage nightmare twice. I've learned to carry all the essentials with me."

She was so naturally, effortlessly beautiful, Mike couldn't imagine she needed much. "I hope our airline didn't lose your luggage," he remarked.

"No." Her silky hair rested just below her shoulders and her eyes paralleled its dark hue. "Neither time," she hastened to inform him.

"Good to hear."

Their gaze held for a moment more. Then she broke it by saying, "Thank you." She started to reach for the bag.

"This is awfully heavy. I'll carry it out for you."

"That's not necessary. I can get it."

"I insist." Mike extended his arm, gesturing for her to walk ahead of him.

She obliged, walking toward the exit on excruciatingly long legs. She stopped at the breezeway and started to say something, but the roar of the vacuums foiled it. She followed his silent direction and when they reached the gate said, "Thanks."

"My pleasure." Mike found himself oddly compelled to make conversation. "Is San Francisco your final destination?" He was torn between not wanting to let her go and not wanting her to miss a connection.

"Yes, I'm in town for a wedding. I also have some business meetings planned for next week. I don't get out to the West Coast very often anymore."

"Anymore?"

"I went to school out here." She sent an expectant glance down to the bag Mike was still holding. "Thank you again, Captain."

He wanted to ask her where, but her tone had become businesslike and he sensed she was ready to be on her way. "Of course. And it's Mike. Mike Savoy." He set the bag at her feet. She smelled as good as she looked.

"Delaney Richards." She extended her hand. "It's nice to meet you, Mike."

"Likewise." Her hand felt as silky smooth as her hair looked. He found himself wanting run his hands through it just to make sure. "Where are you staying?"

The random question seemed to surprise her as much as it had him. "The Fairmont," she informed him.

"Along with being beautiful, you have excellent taste. You can't go wrong there."

"So I've heard." She blushed a little. "Well, I should get to baggage claim before my suitcase goes to lost and found."

Mike laughed without opening his mouth. "You are a seasoned traveler, Ms. Richards."

"Delaney. And yes, I am. The East Coast and Europe for the most part."

"I've traveled the world myself. But there's no place quite like San Francisco." He handed her the bag. "Enjoy your stay."

"I will."

He watched her disappear into the sea of people. He'd never taken such interest in a passenger before. Not that she seemed to mind. She was traveling alone and not wearing an engagement or wedding ring. Maybe he would see her again on her outbound flight. Or better yet in the city. After all, the Fairmont was only a few blocks from his apartment on Nob Hill.

*****

It was after midnight Chicago time when Delaney arrived in her room. But thanks to her cross-country nap, she wouldn't be going to sleep anytime soon. Gazing at the lights meandering up and down Telegraph Hill, she was reminded of how much she loved San Francisco. The clanking of cable cars and bellowing of foghorns brought her back to the days before impossible deadlines, endless meetings and most of all, a broken heart. Of all the things she'd imagined going wrong on her wedding day, finding herself alone at the altar hadn't made the list.

And she hadn't been anywhere near a wedding since.

There'd been plenty of invitations in the last two years, of course. All of which she'd found a convenient reason to decline. But this one was different. This was Lindsay.

They'd gone from randomly assigned room-mates to fast friends in college. Lindsay and Delaney instantly bonded over a myriad of commonalities. Most notably not having a father in their lives, albeit for completely different reasons. Lindsay had lost her parents as a child; Delaney had never known her father. Which made it all the more peculiar that he'd been coming to mind so much lately. She was pushing down the past again when Lindsay's ringtone interrupted her thoughts.

"Welcome back to California." The joy in her friend's voice was palpable.

"Thanks. It's good to be back. How's the bride?"

"Better now that the winds have calmed. The smoke from the brush fires in the foothills made its way up here. Keep your fingers crossed that Saturday will be clear."

"Either way everything will be beautiful," Delaney reassured her.

There was dead air for a long moment, then Lindsay said, "It means so much to me that you came, Laney."

Delaney felt her eyes well with tears. But at least her stomach didn't clench anymore. Or threaten to empty. "I wouldn't miss it for the world," she told her and meant it.

"Can you drive up first thing? That way we can catch-up before everything gets crazy tomorrow night."

"Sure." Delaney assessed her reflection in the full-length mirror with a self-deprecating grimace. "I could use a little Tahoe sun."

"That can be arranged. I was afraid you'd be delayed. Fog shut down SFO for a few hours. You were lucky to have gotten in on time."

She felt a a smile sneak in and reverse the crescent moon-like frown on her mouth. "Yeah, today must be my lucky day."

CHAPTER TWO

THE MORNING SUNLIGHT STREAMING through Mike's bedroom window woke him despite the pillow covering his head. He'd been in the air more than not these last few weeks and had been looking forward to some sleep. So much for that. He grabbed a sweatshirt and went to the kitchen to make coffee. While it brewed, he leafed through a week's worth of mail, assessing what needed to be addressed before the weekend with a operose sigh. This last rotation had been a decidedly long haul. Steaming mug in hand, he scooped up the pertinent mail and went outside. Both sets of French doors opened onto a small deck and today Mike chose the one facing east. He sank into the deck chair as the caws of seagulls and the hum of traffic filled the air. Resting his gaze on the Fairmont, he wondered what Delaney Richards was doing this fine morning.

She'd mentioned being in town for a wedding, presumably this weekend, but didn't say how long into next week she'd be staying. Or whom she'd be staying with, he reminded himself with a grunt. Surely such a beautiful woman wouldn't be at loose ends at a wedding.He was still mulling that over when Bruce Springsteen's gravelly voice filled the air.

"Mr. Savoy?"

"Speaking."

"This is the Hyatt Hotel and Casino Lake Tahoe, calling to confirm your Presidential Suite reservation for tonight."

"That's right." Mike consulted his watch. "I should be there around five o'clock. You have my credit card number for the deposit."

"Yes, that's all been taken care of. I understand this is a bachelor party. There is nothing to indicate that refreshments," the caller cleared his throat as if speaking in code, "or anything else is scheduled to be delivered to the room. Are you planning to enjoy the gaming and restaurants on the property? Or can we bring everything to you, perhaps?"

Chuckling, Mike put the man out of his misery. "That won't be necessary." He was long over that kind of bachelor party as was the groom. "There will only be a few of us. The rehearsal dinner is being held on the property as well, at Hues of Blue. We'll be doing some gambling afterwards. There's no live entertainment, per se."

There was a relieved sigh on the other end of the line. "Very good then. We'll look forward to seeing you this afternoon and accommodating you for the next few days."

Mike responded in kind, then reverted his eyes to the Fairmont. He would probably be too busy over the weekend to give Delaney Richards a second thought. But just in case, he'd better decide where to ask her to dinner when he got back.

*****

Watson Brewer had done his due diligence, but a picture was worth a thousand words. And he didn't want to head up to Folsom until he had something concrete. His plan had been to hop on a plane to Chicago, kill two birds with one stone. But the old lady alone wasn't worth the trek. It was the girl.For a guy who hadn't seen his kid in two decades, Colton Richards sure yapped about her a lot, he snickered to himself. He nodded to the man in the red suit trimmed in gold and opted for the revolving door. The lobby lived up to its reputation, but didn't compare to the Bellagio or the Venetian by a long shot.

"Welcome to the Fairmont. Checking in, sir?"

Watson flashed his best smile. "Just visiting a guest. Delaney Richards. I've forgotten the room number."

"It's against hotel policy to give out room numbers, but I can confirm if the guest is registered. You can use the house phone to contact her." The woman half his age punched at the keyboard on the opposite side of the massive oak desk. Then her smile gave way to a frown. "I'm sorry. Ms. Richards checked out this morning."

Watson swore under his breath, but kept his calculated smile bright. "I'm sure she said she'd be in town through the weekend."

"Perhaps she had a last minute change of plans."

Not according to his source at the airline. He ground his teeth, but didn't let the frustration color his voice. "How odd that she wouldn't have mentioned it. Could there be another reservation?"

The clerk narrowed her eyes in suspicion. "That information is confidential. But if you leave your card, I can pass it along should Ms. Richards return."

"That won't be necessary. I'll find another way to contact her," he replied smoothly. "Thanks for checking." He turned on his heel and retraced his steps, feeling her skeptical stare on his back. Stepping out into the midmorning sunshine, he reached into his jacket pocket and pulled out the photograph. She sure was pretty. Pretty enough to be noticed. He shifted his gaze to the doorman, helping an elderly woman out of a taxi. He'd hoped to fly in a little lower on the radar than that. Questions raise more questions, he reminded himself. And he wanted to be the only asking them.

*****

Lake Tahoe sparkled like diamonds under the boundless blue sky as Delaney entered Incline Village. The estate-like homes shrouded by towering

218

pine trees were as large as the apartment building she'd grown up in, she reminded herself in awe. Reaching her destination, she threw the rental SUV into park and took a couple of deep breaths. She was giving herself props for making it this far when a tap on the window startled her. The eyes looking back at her were as cobalt a blue as the lake itself and the grin as wide as its breadth. Delaney felt the butterflies in her stomach start to settle as she opened the door and stood. Lindsay took her into a warm embrace and hugged her so tight that the two women rocked in place.

"Let me look at you," Lindsay said by way of greeting, giving Delaney a thorough once-over. "Gorgeous as ever, but a little too thin."

"You sound like my mother. I do eat."

With a skeptical squint, she dropped an arm around Delaney's shoulders and led her up the flagstone paved path. "We'll have to work on that this weekend. I can't wait to catch-up. We'll get your bag later."

They reached the two-tiered deck lined with red and white impatiens. "The blue will have to be sky," Lindsay said, reading Delaney's mind. "Note to self, it's impossible to find blue annuals."

"You did all of this yourself?" She took in the perfectly manicured yard, bursting with plants and flowers of all sizes and colors. "When you said you were gardening, I figured you meant a few pots."

"I had to channel my nervous energy somehow. It became a labor of love." Lindsay gestured to one of the chairs circling a slate top table. "Sit. I'll get us something to drink."

"I've been sitting for four hours," Delaney countered, walking to the edge of the deck and imbibing the fresh mountain air. "I'll be right here."

"Suit yourself," Lindsay tossed over her shoulder, blonde ponytail swinging like a pendulum on the back of her head.

Feeling more relaxed than she had in recent memory, Delaney contemplated the water lapping the fawn-colored shore. Her gaze was shifting upward, where rows of pines and aspens dotted the Sierras like soldiers standing at attention when Lindsay returned.

"Amazing how it looks the same, isn't?" Standing next to her, Lindsay handed Delaney a glass of iced tea. "No matter how long you've been away."

"It's magnificent." Delaney took a sip. "A sight for sore eyes from high-rises and strip malls."

"You have a lake in Chicago too, if I remember correctly," Lindsay pointed out with humor shining in her eyes.

"Not like this. I feel like I'm in another world. The air is so crisp, so clean."

"Speaking of clean." Shooting Delaney an pointed stare over the rim of her glass, Lindsay said, "Time for you to."

Delaney played dumb. "Time for me to what?"

"To come clean. You're still not yourself. I could hear it in your voice every time we spoke. What's going on?"

"Nothing's going on," Delaney shot back inadequately.

"Maybe that's the problem. Have you had a night out lately?"

"I'm going to have one tonight, aren't I? And tomorrow night as well."

"I mean a night out with a man." Delaney opened her mouth to speak, but Lindsay barreled over her. "Not business-related. How long has it been?"

"I don't know." Delaney's glance momentarily escaped to the sanctity of the rustic, craftsman-style house. "Is Brian around? I'm dying to meet him."

"He's in Reno picking up his daughter at the airport. Stop trying to change the subject." Lindsay's eyes softened as she went on. "It hurts me to see you like this, letting your life go by. If Ryan walked in here right now, would you forgive him and take him back?"

"No, of course not," Delaney said and meant it.

"Then what are you waiting for? How many dates have you turned down?"

Delaney took a tasteless sip of tea. "None."

"None?" Lindsay amazed. "Are all the men in Chicago blind? Or married?"

"Hardly," Delaney began with a grunt. "I don't really have the time or desire to date. Didn't you feel that way too?"

Lindsay looked away as if mentally rewinding time, then replied heedfully, "Yes, Brian and I both felt that way. That's the difference. Ryan has gone on with his life. You need to do the same." She hesitated, then placing both glasses on the top of the deck railing, took Delaney's hands in hers. "He's not coming back for you, Laney."

"I know." Delaney fixed her eyes on the brown ski runs breaking up the verdant hills. "I realized that even before he eloped." She heaved a sigh. "I don't want him to. I guess somewhere along the way I gave up on true love."

"I did too. So much so that I almost married Paul." She turned Delaney by the shoulders to face her and looked her square in the eye. "I understand what it feels like to love someone that much and lose them. But what you had with Ryan wasn't true love. So your true love is out there somewhere, waiting for you."

*****

Mike pushed the elevator call button repeatedly, frustrated with himself for getting a late start. Lindsay would be frantic by the time he got to the restaurant. Normally he would revel in getting under her skin, but this was different. As was going

222

to a wedding without a date. Even if he and Jessica hadn't called it quits, he wouldn't have asked her to fly in. There were several women he might have asked if the wedding had been in San Francisco. But this was a weekend, not an evening. Too complicated.

Being in Tahoe again, however, was not complicated. Much of his childhood had been spent here, swimming in the lake in the summer and skiing through forests of frost-painted trees in the winter. He'd been thinking about diversifying his investments and buying a place up here would definitely complement his portfolio.

He walked briskly through the lobby, making mental notes of the casino's layout for later. The last fringes of daylight were sliding behind the milky-white peaks of the Sierra Nevadas as he made his way through the lakeside restaurant. He put on an apologetic frown and clasped Brian's shoulders from behind. "Sorry I'm late."

Brian rose and took Mike into a brotherly hug. "No problem. We're just getting started."

"Hi, Uncle Mike," came a soft voice from the table.

Mike bent down and kissed Brian's daughter on the cheek. "Hi, yourself. How's the most beautiful sophomore at USC?"

"I don't know. I'm a technically a junior after the summer session."

"That's impossible. Just last week you were playing Barbies in my living room," he teased. Secretly, that gave Mike pause. Kelsey had grown into a beautiful girl, the splitting image of her mother, with sable hair to Brian's blonde and hazel eyes to his blue.

Brian shifted his proud gaze to the rest of the table. "Mike, you remember Moira Brody."

"Of course." Mike extended his hand to the fair-faced woman with a headful of black ringlet curls. "Nice to see you again."

Instead of shaking it, she jumped up and embraced Mike from across the table. "You too," she replied, emerald eyes sparkling.

The man beside her stood and offered his hand. "Paul Webster. Nice to meet you."

Mike responded in kind and a silent message passed between them. Then his eyes swept the table draped in white linen and glistening china. "Where's Lindsay?"

"Ladies room. She was getting a little restless waiting for the best man," Brian told him with a chuckle in his eyes. "If you don't want wine, go order a beer. My tab is open."

Nodding in affirmation, Mike headed over to the mahogany bar. Brian had the best table in the house tonight, directly in front of the floor-to-ceiling window wall. When Mike looked beyond it, he saw a fire pit surrounded by Adirondack chairs and wooden benches. He was debating how far the deck extended onto the beach when he heard a familiar voice call his name. But when Mike turned around, he found the last person he could have expected. He felt his jaw drop, then blinked hard a few times, assuming she would disappear or morph into someone else.

But she didn't.

Then he realized Lindsay was hugging him. "You made it," she said. "I was getting a little nervous." She broke away and gestured to the woman at her side. "Mike, this is—"

"Delaney Richards," he managed to finish for her.

Lindsay's gaze sliced between them in awe. "You two know each other?"

"I brought her plane in last night."

"And carried my bag out to the gate for me," Delaney added.

"This is the wedding you flew in for?"

A warm smile replaced the astonishment in her eyes. "Lindsay was my roommate in college."

"Brian is my next door neighbor."

"You're the best man?"

Mike could do nothing but nod.

They were still beholding each other when Lindsay cleared her throat and interjected, "Well, I'd better get back to the table." She directed her parting words at Delaney. "I'll meet you there. Take your time."

Delaney's lips parted slightly and she watched Lindsay walk away, as if unsure whether to follow. Not wanting her to, Mike instantly stepped forward. "Can I get you a drink?" She smelled intoxicating; spicy and sexy, akin to the strapless dress she wore.

"No thanks," she declined, meeting his gaze again. "I have a glass of wine at the table."

Mike simply could not take his eyes off of her. After a long moment, Delaney suggested, "We should probably get back there too."

Mike grabbed his beer from the bar and extended his arm. "After you."

She complied, seemingly unaware of the male heads turning to undress her with their eyes as she walked toward the table. Of which Mike was one.

She turned, as if sensing he wasn't behind her, and cocked her head to the side with a puzzled expression. "Mike? Are you coming?"

Mike shook off the stupor and made quick work of the space between them. Then, placing his hand at the small of her back without touching her, he guided her across the room.

There were still three vacant chairs at the table, one with a bird's-eye view of the water and the mountains and two on the opposite side, facing the restaurant. Delaney stopped in front of one of the latter and addressed Kelsey, "Am I losing it, or did you move?"

Before Kelsey could respond, Lindsay piped up. "I asked her to scoot over so we could chat. You don't mind, do you?"

"Of course not." Delaney replied, starting to pull out one of the chairs.

Mike beat her to it. "Here," he offered hurriedly as their arms brushed. He wondered if she'd also felt the dizzying twinge.

"Thanks." She tossed him a look from under her lashes and sat down. And without a second's debate Mike took the chair next to her, opting for the better view.

Read on for a sneak peek of *Last Chance*, the final installment in the *Chances Trilogy* by Martha O'Sullivan

It's finally Paul and Moira's turn...

CHAPTER ONE

The shade hadn't been in her sixty-four count, sharpener-inclusive box of crayons, but Moira Brody had known it for as long as she could remember. Saturating the cloudless sky, it hung behind the Sierra Nevadas like a boundless blue curtain, encompassing the milky peaks and snow-clad pines before yielding to the preternatural liquid hue that was Lake Tahoe. Moira's boots crunched on the snowpack as she welcomed the blast of crisp air that replaced the arid closeness she'd been breathing for the last hour. Inhaling antidotally, she aimed her gait at the freshly shoveled path. She knocked and opened the door at the same time. "Linds?"

"Up here."

Moira stomped the snow off her boots, then shed them and her coat before following the sound of footfalls upstairs. The smell of fresh wood and lemon beeswax drew her to the bedroom at the end of the hall. There she found Lindsay Rembrandt contemplating three paint swatches taped to the wall.

"What do you think?" Lindsay asked by way of greeting, blonde ponytail swinging like a pendulum at the back of her head. "Muted Mint, Seafoam Spray or Green Tea?"

"You're the interior designer, not me." Moira walked over to the wall in question, drenched in bright winter sunshine. After a moment's consideration she replied, "Muted Mint, not that it matters."

Lindsay immediately straightened her shoulders and knitted her brow. "Why wouldn't it matter?"

"Because," Moira answered, feeling the inner smile spread across her mouth. "When that baby girl is born, you're going to repaint. You should be looking at pink paint strips."

Lindsay's cobalt blue eyes narrowed with intrigue. "What makes you so sure it's a girl anyway?"

"Gut," Moira told her. "And you deserve a girl. You always wanted a sister."

"I thought I had one," Lindsay reminded her gently.

"You know what I mean," Moira returned in kind.

"Brian and I just want a healthy baby," she maintained, but the delight on her face intensified. "Besides, we already have Kelsey."

"Kelsey's nearly out of college. You could be a step-grandmother in a few years."

"Bite your tongue." Lindsay broke their shared gaze and reverted to the task at hand, giving Moira a profile view of her second trimester baby bump. "Good call with the Muted Mint, though. That's what we're painting the nursery at home. It seems silly to have one at each house, but I feel so close to Gram here. I want her to be a part of it."

"She'd be so happy for you, Linds. And so proud."

"I know." She brushed her fingertips under her lower lashes. "Damn hormones. I don't have a thing to cry about."

"Emily was the same way. And the cravings," Moira went on theatrically, waving her hand in the air. "Jack was forever running to Raley's in the middle of the night."

"How are the twins?"

"Great. I'm babysitting them on Friday night. They're starting to—"

"You're babysitting your nephews on Valentine's Day?" Spinning back around, Lindsay cut her off.

"Yeah."

"With Paul?"

"No."

"Why?"

"Because Jack and Emily hardly ever get an evening out, let alone an overnight."

"Why aren't you doing something with Paul on Valentine's Day?" Lindsay's tone was a mixture of disappointment and confusion.

Moira had wondered the same, but kept that to herself. "He hasn't mentioned anything. And you know how hard it is to find a babysitter on Valentine's Day," she hesitated, then added, "I offered."

"You offered?" Lindsay repeated in open-mouthed wonder.

"Yeah, I stayed with the boys last year."

"But everything was different then!"

"It certainly was. They were barely walking. And you weren't married, let alone pregnant."

"I mean with you and Paul and you know it!"

Moira started with a tired breath, "Linds…"

"Did you break up?"

"No. We weren't really all the way together. "

"You looked pretty together at my wedding," Lindsay pointed out.

"That was six months ago."

"I knew something was up. You skirted the issue every time I mentioned it. Shame on me for not putting two and two together sooner."

"Yeah, because between remodeling a house, going back to school and having a baby you should have been more on top of my love life. All while living four hours away."

Lindsay ignored Moira's attempt at sarcasm and taking her hands, said in earnest, "I'm sorry, Moirs. I didn't realize it was so…" she searched for the word, "casual between the two of you."

"Me neither." Moira's heart caught up with her mouth and she finished quietly, "It is what it is."

"And what is that exactly?"

"What it's always been. Friendship. Familiarity. History. Maybe that's all it's supposed to be," Moira told her with borrowed conviction.

"Yeah," Lindsay allowed with a skeptical shake of the head. "Maybe."

"Now, show me the pink swatches you picked up."

Lindsay shot her a measured look, but relented, "You know me too well."

"Likewise," Moira replied, also knowing the matter was far from laid to rest.

*****

"It's not like she owes me an explanation or anything," Paul Webster told Jack Brody later that afternoon. "I'm just surprised."

"I was too when she offered," Jack said from across his cluttered desk. "But I've learned not to ask too many questions of the women in my life. Beginning with my sister and ending with my wife."

Suddenly uncomfortable, Paul shifted in his seat and released a jagged breath. He'd gotten into the habit of taking Moira for granted, he supposed. But not to the tugging feeling in the pit of his stomach when he let himself think too much about her. "Where is she anyway?"

"Up at the lake. Lindsay's in town. They're picking out paint or curtains or something," Jack informed him with a dismissive wave.

"Figures."

"So what's the deal with you two anyway?" Jack asked. "Is it an on-again, off-again thing?"

"No." Paul found himself oddly offended. "There is no deal. It's Moira for God's sake. Sometimes it's just a little weird. Almost like dating your sister."

"Actually, it *is* dating my sister." Jack's hazel eyes clouded. "Don't break her heart or anything. Hate to say it, but blood is thicker than water. Even though you literally saved my life in the latter."

Jack ended on a light note, but Paul noted the nuance of his words. "It's not like that. We stumbled into I don't know what, and then right back out again. Hell, I'm in Portland nearly every week now and playing catch-up in the office on the weekends."

Jack silenced his half-assed explanation with a decided hand. "Emily thought I should talk to you before we made any definite Valentine's Day plans. In case you were planning a surprise."

Paul leaned forward in an attempt to settle the restlessness swirling inside him. "What kind of surprise?"

Jack shrugged. "Dinner, flowers, little gifts. All that stuff I used to do before I got married."

Paul had done all that stuff too…for Lindsay, he reminded himself with a mental kick. But everything with Moira was different. Easy, casual, familiar. Wooing her didn't even occur to him. Should it? He sure as hell didn't like the idea of wooing her occurring to someone else.

"So can I tell my hopelessly romantic wife that we have a night to ourselves?" Jack's eyes danced hopefully.

"Only if she finds another babysitter," Paul heard himself say. "Moira has plans."

CHAPTER TWO

"Happy Valentine's Day."

Moira lifted her eyes from the computer monitor in the direction of the familiar voice. "Happy Valentine's Day to you." She marked her place on the spreadsheet and pushed up from behind her desk. "I didn't expect to see you today."

"I was in the area unexpectedly. Thought I'd drop by my best account."

"Brody and Sons Construction is your best account, huh?" she challenged around a laugh.

"Okay," Jason Parker conceded affably. "My favorite account. I had a meeting down the block." He took in the open-air office asking, "Is Jack around?"

"Jack is never around on paydays or Friday afternoons. Today is both."

Jason's chiseled jaw relaxed, allowing his loose male grin to advertise his movie star white teeth. "That's right. I've heard how your Irish temper comes out when you do the books."

"Small business ownership is a perpetual roller coaster. Business is strong but supply chain remains a challenge. It's a domino effect."

"Same here."

Moira returned the cordial, lingering smile, but intuition told her Jason Parker had more than windows on his mind. And she wasn't sure how she felt about that. After a few silent beats she put in, "I'll tell Jack you stopped by."

Jason didn't respond, only gave her a meditative nod. Then his expression tightened and Moira could almost see his heart begin to race inside his chest. "So, what are you up to tonight? Big Valentine's Day plans?" His blue eyes swept the office, then rested on Moira's desk as if searching for something. Like flowers. Or a chocolate heart. Or anything to denote Valentine's Day.

Moira willed the heat rushing through her body not to settle in her cheeks. She cleared her throat and commended herself for having the inadvertent foresight to keep the reception counter between them. Then she answered in a voice higher than she would have liked, "Me? Oh, no. Someone has to keep the lights on around here, you know," she told him, gesturing to her desk. "And people expect to be paid, Valentine's Day or not."

That seemed to surprise, then please him. The confident countenance returned and rested squarely on the broad shoulders supporting his suit coat. "How about dinner, then? Everything decent is probably booked, but we could go a little later, after the rush," he offered with building enthusiasm. "That would give you time to finish up. Or we could get take-out and eat it here."

Grateful Jason didn't suggest take-out at his place, Moira began a weak internal debate. Her conversation with Paul the day before yesterday had been brief and in response to a butt call on his part. He hadn't said anything about Valentine's Day or the weekend. Emily had come down with the flu, so she and Jack were staying home. And Lindsay had gone back to San Francisco.

"You have to eat, one way or the other," Jason was still talking.

She met his expectant stare head-on. There was no reason not to accept his heartfelt invitation. "Take-out would be great," she decided out loud.

"Then it's a date," he triumphed. "Think about what you'd like to eat. I'll touch base in a few hours."

Moira pushed back the bittersweet twinges nipping at her stomach and managed an oblique smile. "Anything is fine. Surprise me."

*****

Paul mumbled under his breath and patted his pockets. He must have left his phone in the car. He cast his gaze upward, letting the sun's position on the horizon confirm his suspicions that he was running late. The florist closed at six o'clock, Valentine's Day or not, he'd been told when placing his order. The clerk had also remarked that at this late juncture, his only saving grace was that he didn't want roses. And that was not by accident.

He'd given Lindsay and every other woman he'd dated roses, but Moira was more of a hydrangea or a lily than a rose. Not that he'd ever given her flowers before, he self-admonished as that ineffable feeling began engulfing his gut again. He picked up his pace and arrived at the florist in less than five minutes. The dry heat billowed out into the damp winter air the second he opened the shop door, biting at his cheeks. He got in line and began to mentally review his plan. Every restaurant in town was booked solid by the time he'd tried to make a reservation, but Moira was easy to please and take-out would surely due. The tricky part would be tearing her away from work so close to the fifteenth of the month.

He was ruminating on his midweek conversation with Jack for the umpteenth time when he heard an orotund voice behind him point out, "I think it's your turn."

Returning to the present, Paul threw an apology over his shoulder and stepped forward.

"No problem," the man replied. "I'm in no hurry myself, but the guy behind me is sweating bullets. Once you're in, you're in, I told him. Florists want to make money just like the rest of us."

Nodding in agreement, Paul turned his attention to the person addressing him from behind the counter.

"Picking up, sir?"

"Yeah. Webster."

The perky teenager punched at the keyboard and consulted the computer monitor. "One Spring Splash bouquet, substitute roses." She hit a few more keys, then handed Paul a receipt. "They'll bring it right up."

Paul followed her silent direction and stepped aside. The customer behind him advanced and started with a sigh, "I know it's slim pickings, but are there any red roses left?"

"I'm sorry, sir," the girl apologized with the inklings of a smirk. "We're sold out of red roses, but have an array of other flowers. We could arrange something lovely for you."

Undaunted by what should be a less than startling revelation, the man rounded his cheeks conspiratorially. "Surely there must be something in the back? Even some imperfects? This is a first date; someone I've been interested in for some time. I don't want to blow it."

"We don't discount; the owner is very particular," she explained with a more compassionate smile. "But I could double-check the cuttings. You'll have to wait until I fill all these orders, though." She tipped her head at the dozen man deep line. "It might be a few minutes."

"No problem. She's working late anyway." The man joined Paul next to the near-empty glass door cooler. "I guess cuttings are better than nothing," he said around a shrug.

"I'm sure they'll find you something," Paul encouraged, feeling sorry for the complete stranger. "Might not be red roses though."

"I knew that would be a long shot."

"I wish I could have given you mine. I had them switched out."

"You're kidding," he responded with a jolt. "What woman doesn't like roses? Especially on Valentine's Day?"

"It's not that she wouldn't like them. They just don't suit her."

The man laughed without opening his mouth. "For your sake I hope not."

Just then a woman appeared from behind the counter calling, "Mr. Webster?"

"Right here."

Stepping forward, Paul took the cellophane wrapped bouquet from her hands. "Thanks."

"My pleasure."

Turning around, he shot his new acquaintance a tight nod. "Good luck."

"Same to you."

Suddenly dismayed by the thought he would need it, Paul turned on his heel and walked out into the brisk night. It was full dark now and the headlights gleaming off the wet pavement reminded him of his next stop. He wondered if Moira would be as surprised to receive the gift as he'd been to buy it.

But he'd felt as compelled to purchase it as he had been to be with her tonight. He'd held up his part of the deal, whatever the deal was. The rest was up to her.

CHAPTER THREE

MOIRA PUSHED HER SIDE-SWEPT bangs out of her eyes and blew out her third calming breath. She'd flown through payroll before running home to change and freshen up. Now she was back at the office with the intention of reconciling the ledgers. Instead, she was contemplating herself in the full-length mirror on the back of the bathroom door for at least the fifth time. She hadn't wanted to wear the distressed jeans and cotton sweater she'd thrown on this morning, but didn't want to try too hard either. A dress was out of the question and presumptuous, not that she had anything appropriate anyway. So she'd chosen the floral blouse she'd bought on her last trip to San Francisco and skinny jeans with a little bling on the back pockets. The outfit had been the easy part; the shoes were the problem. She glanced from one foot to the other, each modeling an option. Boots were casual and sexy. Heels were stylish and sexy. Both sent a message—a sexy one. But Moira wasn't sure sexy was the message she wanted to send.

She hadn't had a date, first or otherwise, in ages. Lindsay's wedding had been as close to a real date as she and Paul had gotten, Moira supposed. Aside from that it was going here and there, seeing a movie, attending an event or a family function. None of which were ever followed by anything more than a parting good night kiss.

Except for that night.

That kiss, or kisses, she corrected herself, had been the first time there'd been more, much more. The first time the pull in her stomach had crept downward and settled between her thighs. The first time the buzzing in her head had spread to every cell in her body and exploded. The first time the steady canter of her heartbeat became a hastening gallop. But not the first time Paul backed off and said good night. That happened every time. Not that she would have wanted to lose her virginity in such a wine-induced state anyway, she grunted under her breath. And to all people, Paul Webster, her ninth grade lab partner and brother's best friend. Yes she did, she thought, grimacing at her reflection. But of late Paul had been aloof, indifferent, busy. And in Portland half the time.

Jason Parker, however, the ash-blond, spring ski-tanned, five o'clock-shadowed window salesman was in her office every month. And he seemed genuinely excited about spending the evening with her. And not just any evening. Valentine's Day. A Valentine's Day date. Jason had said so himself. Her thoughts were returning to her footwear dilemma when she heard the door chimes ring. "Shit!" she swore under her breath, pushing down the melancholy. She kicked off the chunky heel and tugged

244

on the other pump boot, then indulged herself with another quick glance in the mirror. Scrunching the teeming curls she'd grown up hating, she squared her shoulders and painted on a smile. But when Moira emerged with a cheery greeting on her lips, she found the office just as empty as she had left it. Except for the artfully arranged bouquet of red roses cradled in white carnations sitting on the counter. She discharged a shotgun breath. This was definitely a date. The rosebuds were small and the stems short, peeking out of the hourglass-shaped vase girdled with a red velvet bow. She was leaning down to sniff one when she realized Jason was standing in the doorway watching her. Shuffling back a step, she threw an alarmed hand to her chest. "Oh! I didn't see you there."

He took the two remaining strides to complete his entry and approached her. "Sorry. I didn't mean to startle you. I dropped those off and ran back out to the car for the food." His appreciative gaze took her in from head to toe. "Happy Valentine's Day, Moira. You look incredible."

"Thanks. You too."

He'd traded his dress shirt and tie for a casual button-down and dress pants for slim-fitting jeans. He was standing within a few breaths of her now with a blank look on his face, seeming to debate something. Like kissing her.

Admittedly only partly relieved when he didn't, she shifted her gaze back to the flowers. "The roses are beautiful. Thank you."

"My pleasure. And my second lucky break of the day," he told her. "By the time I got to the florist, they were already sold out. I talked the clerk into selling me the day's cuttings."

How sweet, Moira thought. That sounded like something Paul would do. For Lindsay. She cleared the past from her throat. "I bet they were slammed."

"As advertised. So was Bernini's." He raised his arms to the elbows, displaying two brown shopping bags. "I took the safe route with Italian. Hope that's okay."

"Perfect. I haven't eaten all day. Where do you want to sit?" she asked, gesturing around the room with her hand. "We don't really have an eating area. Just a kitchenette in the back."

He gave the office an appraising once-over, then rested his gaze on the desk in the corner. "Want to pull up another chair over there?"

The desk was in abeyance, but cleared off thanks to Lindsay pretending she was over Brian summer before last. Being Paul's biggest fan, she'd be furious to know it went to such use. Moira snickered to herself. "Sure."

"So, did you get the books done?" Jason asked, setting down the bags and hanging his leather jacket on the back of the desk chair. A woodsy, gingery scent wafted through the air and formed a steady current under Moira's nose.

"Almost," she answered as they opened the foiled-covered containers. "Payroll is sent and that's the most important thing. I can always reconcile over the weekend."

His eyes filled with understanding and she could almost see the wheels turning in his head. "Do you work a lot on the weekends?"

"Lately it seems. First world problems. How about you?"

"Yeah. Paperwork, paperwork. Or should I say paperless work? But either way, I'd rather be skiing or boarding." His voice trailed off and he pulled two wine bottles out of the second bag. "Which do you prefer?"

"Skiing," she told him, relaxing a little. "My eye-hand coordination is better than my sense of balance."

Chuckling, he glanced down. "I'll keep that in mind. But I meant red or white?" He displayed a bottle of each.

Moira felt her cheeks burst into flame. "Oh," she faltered. "Red would be great. Do you need a corkscrew? I think there's one back there."

"No," Jason declined, producing one. "Got that covered. Just some glasses."

"Sure."

Moira started to walk away, but Jason caught her arm and said, "I'm really glad you agreed to have dinner with me, especially tonight. I was almost afraid to ask."

"I'm glad you did," Moira affirmed, hoping she sounded more sincere than she felt inside. He really was a nice guy. She left him with a closemouthed smile and headed for the kitchen. All she could find was plastic cups, but they would have to do. She considered bringing out the candles they kept around for emergencies, but thought better of it. She didn't want to come on too strong and give Jason the wrong impression. And no matter how hard she tried, she couldn't get Paul out of her mind. What was he doing tonight, she wondered?

So when she returned to the front a few minutes later and found him just inside the threshold of the door, she blinked hard a couple of times, thinking her eyes were playing tricks on her. There were a few seconds of shared consternation as she watched him stand there, rooted in pie-eyed wonder, slicing his astonished stare between Jason and her.

It was a good thing Solo cups were all Moira could find, because they immediately fell through her splaying fingers. They struck the tile floor, one clangorous bounce at a time, then rolled away. Frozen in the inertia of disbelief, she could only let them go and bring a shocked hand to her mouth. It took her three reflective beats to process the flowers in Paul's left hand, the bottle of wine in his right. Then her prickling eyes reunited with his caramel-colored ones. His were stormy, full of confusion and awe. And bygone scars. Guilty satisfaction joined the shock and wound into a tight braid of angst in her stomach. Finally, she stammered, "Paul, what are you doing here?"

"I could ask you the same question," he replied derisively.

There was a long, heavy silence during which Moira fought an overwhelming urge to run away. She was still striving for calm when she heard Jason clear his throat uneasily and announce, "I'll just go grab some napkins from the back."

With a grateful nod Moira waited for him leave, then answered Paul loftily, "I'm having dinner."

"I can see that." His voice clipped. "With whom?"

"A friend."

Paul's sable brows furrowed suspiciously. "I don't know him."

"You don't know all my friends," she told him, sniffing the air.

"Obviously."

"Besides, he's a new friend."

"Dinner with a new friend. On Valentine's Day," he disdained. "How quaint."

"I didn't have any other plans, did I?" Her voice suddenly sounded more pitiful than she would have liked.

Paul's posture stiffened and he closed the distance between them with three calculated strides.

"What kind of a friend is he?" he demanded as the smell of anise replaced its outdoorsy predecessor.

"Just a friend," she told him with an assumptive shrug, noticing for the first time that he was dressed up.

"Then what am I?"

There was a moment so quiet Moira could hear static crackling in the air. Finally she broke it. "I don't know. A friend I've hardly seen or spoken to much lately."

Paul's expression softened a little, like he already knew that. And it bothered him.

"I see. So how long have you and..."

"Jason," Moira finished for him, trying to ignore the familiar, intoxicating scent filling the small space between them.

"Jason," he began again, "been friends?"

"He's called on us for the last year or two."

"Oh, so he's a work friend? No wonder," Paul disparaged. "He wouldn't know that you don't like the sauce at Bernini's. It's too sweet." He shifted his gaze to the salad Jason had split between their plates. "And that you don't care for black olives."

Moira raised her chin a notch. "I can pick them off. And no, he wouldn't know that. It's our first date," she countered sharply.

"So it *is* a date?" Paul returned to her with flinty eyes and a corded neck. "A first date on Valentine's Day. How sweet," he sneered. "And to think I was

250

worried about tearing you away from your spread-sheets in the middle of the month."

"Tear me away for what?" she couldn't help but ask.

"Dinner, for starters." Flippant now, he noted the clock on the wall. "It should be here anytime." Then his regard settled on the bouquet in his hand, as if just remembering he was holding it. He deliberated for a few seconds before setting it on her desk with a resounding thud. "I'll leave these here, seeing how the front counter is crowded."

"Paul—"

"I'll hang on to the Cakebread, though," he plowed over her. "It's too good of a year to waste."

He started for the door, but turned on his heel mid-stride to face her again. "Funny. I never pegged you for roses. Too ostentatious. But I guess I was wrong about that too. Happy Valentine's Day, Moira."

The braid in her stomach unwound into strands of dread as she watched him swing the door open and storm out into the night. Beside herself, she could only stand there in stunned silence, hand on her breastbone and tears stinging her eyes.

"Is it safe to come out now?" came a tentative voice from somewhere in the back.

Suddenly remembering Jason was still there, she spun around in complete mortification. "Yes, of course. I'm so sorry. We just had a little...miscommunication."

"Looks like more than that to me," Jason contended mildly. "Maybe I should go."

"No!" she exclaimed in short order. "Please don't. This is all so lovely. I'd really like you to stay. I mean..." She wrung her hands. "If you still want to. But I understand if you don't."

"I do," he told her quietly, then approached her with eyes full of trepidation. "I just don't want to get in the way."

"You couldn't." Moira noted the weight of his words and shaking her head slowly from side to side, matched it. "Because there isn't anything to get in the way of."

CHAPTER FOUR

THE BLACK ICE CAST an eerie sheen on the road ahead and the glare from the oncoming high beams had Paul squinting as if at the summer sun. The weather was coming in fast and he wondered if Moira had gotten home safely.

Or alone.

Or at all.

He should have gotten her roses. But he didn't. Because she's Moira. Effortlessly beautiful, remarkably grounded, perpetually good-natured Moira. And tonight she was something else. Incredibly sexy. In tight-fitting jeans and a silky top he'd never seen before. With her dark, thick, begging to be touched curls skimming her shoulders. And eye makeup and red lipstick. She smelled pretty good too. Like spring rain and lilacs. All for the guy begging for roses at the flower shop. For someone he'd been "interested in for some time." For whom he had a last minute arrangement thrown together. From *his* cuttings. For *his* girl. Paul huffed out a harried breath. Is that what she was? Apparently not. But he sure as hell wanted her to be. He slammed on the brakes and the SUV swerved, then leveled, sliding into the precarious U-turn.

It took Paul twice as long as usual to get back to Reno with the slick roads. And by then the temperature had dropped enough to turn the spitting rain into steely pellets. A frigid, damp sleet akin to the block of ice that had staked a claim in the pit of his stomach. Turning the corner onto Moira's street, he heaved a half-hearted sigh of relief when he saw no car in the driveway and a hodgepodge of lights burning inside. She was home. Alone it would seem.

Unless they came in one car, he prepared himself through gritted teeth.

Paul knew the garage code, but didn't want to scare her, so he opted for the conventional route. He could see her profile through the slats of the plantation shutters as he made his way up the path to the front door. She was in the kitchen fussing with something, still dressed up like she hadn't been home long. His throat muscles contracted as his mind began to race. Had her date seen her home or had they parted ways at the office? Gone somewhere for a drink after dinner? Made another date? He looked on as Moira stepped back from the kitchen island, arms drawn across her chest, and appraised her work. The fancy jeans sat just below her hips, hugging every one of her curves from hip to ankle and Paul found himself disturbingly envious. The sheer shirt rested on her slim waist and reminded him of holding her in his arms when they danced at Lindsay's wedding. And her breasts looked bigger somehow, like they'd grown over-night. The mere thought of touching them made his heart skip a beat and his cock begin to swell.

Seemingly pleased with her work, she reached for the dish towel flung over her shoulder and dried her hands, inadvertently catching a glimpse of him out of the corner of her eye. She did a double take, then held his gaze momentarily. He thought the corners of her mouth curved slightly upward, but the distance between them was too great to be sure. She shook off whatever she was thinking and walked toward the door. He visualized her on the other side, squeezing her eyes shut and taking a few deep breaths before opening it. She greeted him in a wobbly voice, "Hey."

She looked mesmerizing in the amber light. Her emerald green eyes were soulful and clung to his as if unwittingly attached. Her full lips were naked now and Paul told himself it was from eating. The coal-black tendrils had doubled, the errant strands falling in sexy waves around her fair face. Also from natural causes, he told himself. "Hey. Can I come in?"

"Of course," she invited, ushering him in.

Stepping inside, Paul rapid-fired, "I'm glad you're home. I wanted to—"

"Where else would I be at eleven o'clock at night?" she cut him off.

"I don't know." His mind was suddenly a mare's nest and his palms were beginning to sweat. "I wasn't sure what your plans were for the rest of the evening."

"I've been home for almost an hour," she informed him evenly.

"Alone?" His eyes scanned the living room.

"It was just dinner, Paul," Moira patronized.

On Valentine's Day, he silently added. "About that, I came by to apologize." He wondered if she sensed the audible relief in his voice. "I shouldn't have assumed we'd see each other tonight. And I certainly shouldn't have assumed you'd be," he bit off the word, "available." He looked away then, into the kitchen, and saw what she'd been doing. Arranging flowers.

His flowers.

She must have acquired clairvoyant powers in those few seconds, because her tone softened and she said, "I had to bring them home. They're too beautiful to waste."

With four long strides he advanced into the kitchen and glanced around. "Where are the roses?"

She followed him. "At the office."

"They're not too beautiful to waste?" he asked in a thick voice, turning to face her.

"No, they are." Her breath hitched. "They're just not from you."

Her eyes were filling behind their dark lashes and she was biting her bottom lip, trying to hold back the tears. Paul couldn't have stopped himself from going to her if he'd wanted to. "Moira, what are we doing?" he implored, gripping her forearms. "What have I done? Have I lost you?"

She shook her head from side to side and the tears began to fall, leaving sooty tracks on her cheeks. Tipping his head back in silent gratitude, Paul gathered her in his arms. She instantly moved into his body, sniffling through sawed-off breaths.

"Tell me nothing happened. Tell me there's nothing between you and him," he prayed out loud after a long moment.

She answered by burrowing her head into his shoulder and wreathing his middle. He felt her breathing level and he kissed the top of her head. She smelled like a subtle version of earlier, infused with wine and garlic. Hope replaced the trepidation in his stomach and he heard himself say, "I had to force myself not to go back there. I've been driving around for hours, going crazy."

She angled out of his grasp just enough to make eye contact. Suddenly she was the girl he used to know again, not the woman tying his insides into knots. Or maybe the perfect combination of both. Her eyes began to shine and a satisfied smile curved her lips. "You have?"

"Yeah. Like outside my mind crazy." He laid his lips on hers and tasted the salt from her tears. She melted into the kiss, then the next. He wondered if she could sense him growing behind the zipper. Or the spool of want unwinding into a thousand frazzled threads in his gut. Gasping for air, he released her mouth and cupped her face in his hands. "You make me crazy, Moira Brody. Absolutely crazy."

Her breath caught in her throat and she swallowed hard. "Then I like you crazy."

Resting his forehead on hers, he let the night roll off his back like sweat. Then he closed his eyes and asked, "Do I need to fight for you, Moira?"

She laughed a little. "Well, Jason did bring flowers, dinner, wine."

"I brought flowers, dinner, wine," Paul defended high-mindedly, straightening. "Did you ever get the Chinese food?"

"Yeah, it's in there." She nodded over his shoulder at the sub-zero refrigerator they'd picked out together.

"It's your favorite. Cashew chicken."

"Thank God," she said lightly, dabbing the outer corners of her eyes. "I'm starving."

Paul sent her a confused look. "Did Bernini's have a bad night?"

"Not from what I picked at."

"Poor guy," he gloated through a chuckle. "Went to all that trouble for nothing."

"I wouldn't say for nothing," Moira demurred, her eyes dancing with innuendo. "He seemed to enjoy the evening."

"Oh?" Paul inquired, stepping out of her embrace.

Beaming now, she raised her eyebrows mischievously. "Yeah."

He felt his expression fall. "Did he kiss you good night?"

"He did," Moira preened.

Paul couldn't believe how much that bothered him. "Did you want him to?"

Her face instantly sobered. "No," she paused, then finished with hushed care, "I wanted you to come back."

"I did." As if he'd had any choice in the matter. Paul drew her to him again and ran his hands up and down her back. "I had to."

"That was all I could think about during dinner," she admitted into the crook of his shoulder. "That I could have spent Valentine's Day with you."

"It's not over quite yet." He leaned back and dried her tearstained cheeks with his thumbs. "Think he'll call you?"

She shrugged matter-of-factly. "Yeah."

"What will you say?"

"What should I say?"

"Thanks, but no thanks." He reached into his jacket pocket.

Her eyes narrowed in confusion as she took the small box from his open hands. "Paul, what is this?"

He gestured toward the bow-topped lid with a tip of the head. "Open it and find out."

Moira obliged as Paul looked on eagerly. A tiny gasp escaped her throat when she saw the diamond studs inside.

"I know they're on the small side, but you aren't one for flash."

She glided her fingertips over each diamond. "They're beautiful."

"Emily thought they were perfect." Just like you, he almost said.

Her astonished gaze shifted upward. "Emily?"

"She's not sick. She found another sitter for tonight." He paused to let the benevolent betrayal sink in. "So we could spend Valentine's Day together."

"Oh, Paul! I'm so sorry!" Moira exclaimed. "I had no idea."

Neither did he. Until just now. And the realization hit him like a ton of bricks. "You can make it up to me tomorrow night," he told her on the fly. "We're going on a date. It'll be our first one."